WE JUST COULDN'T SAY GOODBYE

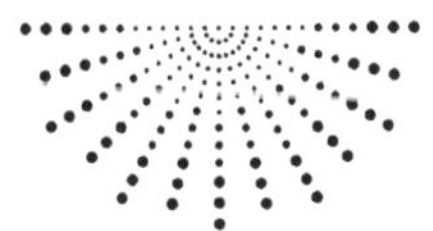

LAYNE DEEMER

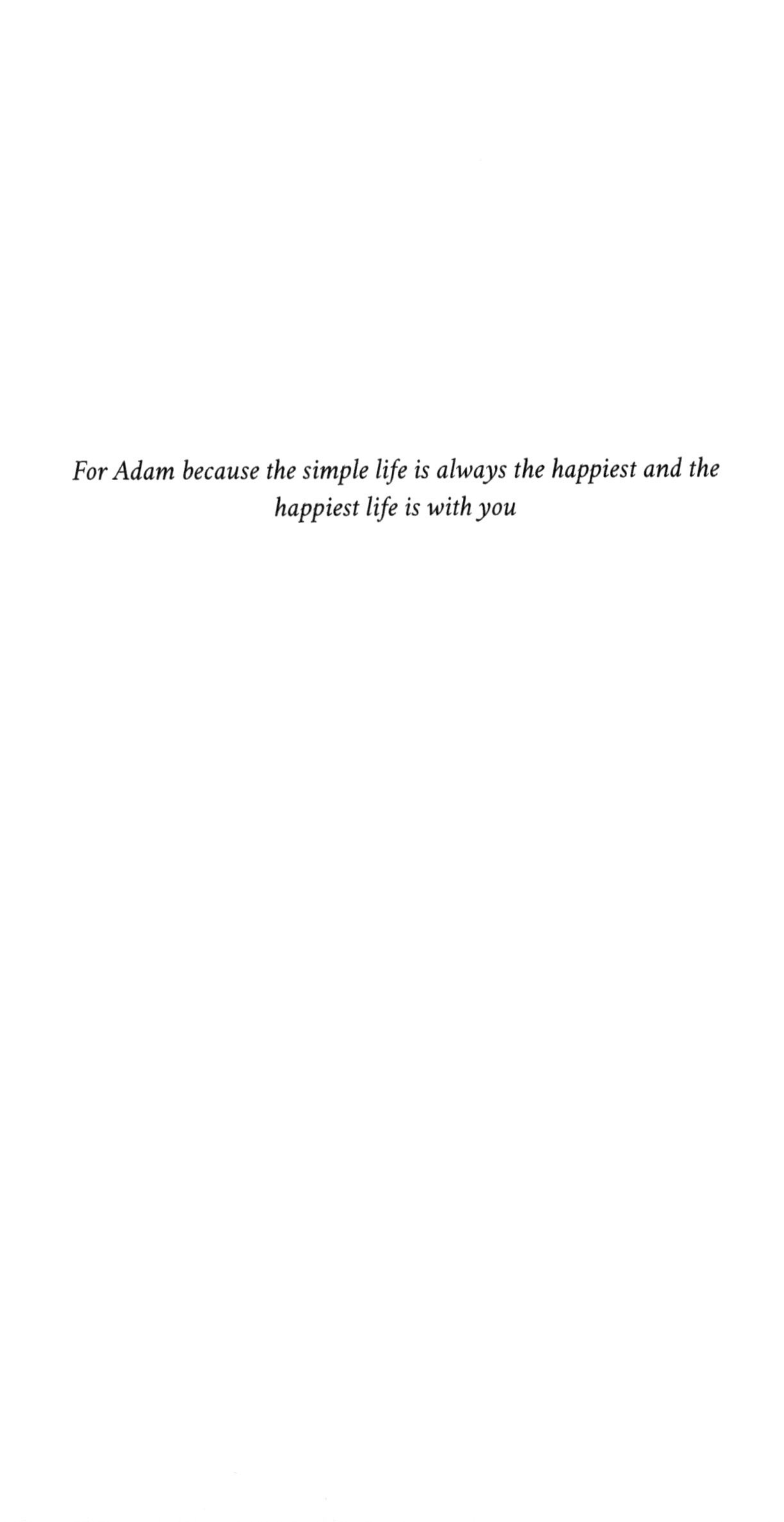

For Adam because the simple life is always the happiest and the happiest life is with you

AUTHOR'S NOTE

This story was inspired by a playlist I discovered on Spotify. The moment I started listening to it, these characters came to life in my head and I put everything else on hold while I told their story. If you want to listen to Cole and Sylvie's music, you can find it on Spotify. https://tinyurl.com/dt8dn76c

Please note, due to adult content, my books are recommended for readers age 18 or older.

For a detailed list of content/trigger warnings, please visit my website. https://www.laynedeemer.com/warnings

Thank you!

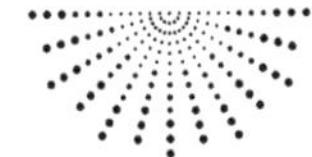

CHAPTER ONE

"Careful!" I call out to the elderly man beside me. He was about to plunge his foot into a puddle, but thankfully, I caught him in time. He smiles and turns the corner, giving me a wave over his shoulder. I grin, feeling like I've done my good deed for the day.

But no good deed goes unpunished.

As I approach the road, a blue minivan comes careening around the corner. Its back tire dips toward the curb and into the tiny river of water flowing toward the storm drain. I'm standing too close, but I have no time to react as a spray of dark, polluted rainwater flies out of the street and onto my leg, where it runs down into my shoe.

"Well, that's just perfect," I mutter.

The van continues driving, unaware of the destruction left in its wake. Or maybe they saw it all. Maybe they're filming me right now, and I'll be the next viral video.

I can see it now. WOMAN STANDS LIKE A DROWNED RAT AFTER GETTING PELTED WITH RAINWATER

Fantastic.

How am I supposed to go to work like this? If Jackie sees

me, I'll never hear the end of it. But I'm too far away from home to turn back. If I do, I'll never make it in time.

I stand motionless on the sidewalk, ticking my head back and forth like the pendulum of a clock. I could go home and call in and say I'm running late.

Jackie would have a field day with that.

No, I'm not giving her the ammunition. She's had her eye on my corner office ever since I moved in last month. She's been hard at work, trying to find an angle to weasel in and swipe it from me.

But I can't show up looking like this. I need to at least dry off.

I hear the faint sounds of old music. The kind with muted trumpets and a slow, even tempo. It takes me a moment to figure out where it's coming from, but I follow the sound across the street and stop in front of a small brick cafe with a wide, curtained window and a quaint little sign that reads Cole's Cafe.

Funny. I've never noticed it before, but I don't usually walk to work this way. My normal route is under construction, and I was catcalled enough yesterday to last me a lifetime.

I'm sure this cafe must have a bathroom. I could pop in and attempt to dry off my leg and try to salvage my leather Mary Jane.

When I push the door open, I'm not at all surprised to hear a little bell. This is exactly the sort of place that would have that detail. I give the interior a once-over, finding it cozy and warm. It's also rather empty at the moment, which is a little mortifying for me. I had hoped to not call much attention to myself, planning to slip into the bathroom and back out without being noticed, or at least only marginally noticed.

There's a row of small round tables along the wall, each

with two chairs pushed into them. A long white counter lines the right of the cafe. Actually, it takes up the entire wall. I'm not sure I've ever seen such a lengthy counter. Round silver stools with bright orange cushions are dotted around the counter. They're the kind that have been cemented into the ground, and I bet if I sat on one, it would spin.

"Hi there, miss. What can I get for ya?" a rich, deep voice calls from somewhere behind the counter. I'm a bit stunned because I didn't notice anyone when I first walked in. And now that I'm looking, I still don't.

"Um, hello?"

A man pops up with a rag in his hand. He's wearing a white apron and a dazzling grin. "Sorry. I was just filling up the ice tray," he tells me while running the white rag along the counter in wide circles.

My smile is shy when I respond. "I didn't see you there when I came in."

He smiles back, but there's nothing timid about him. "What can I get started for you?"

"Oh, uh," I stammer, resting a shaky hand over my rapidly beating heart. "I was actually just hoping to use your restroom." I wince as the words leave my mouth. This place is empty, and I've never seen it before. Maybe it's new. Maybe I'm his first customer, and here I am, just asking where the toilets are.

"Sure thing. It's just straight back and on your right," he says, not missing a beat.

Maybe I'm overthinking it. But that's kind of what I do—always creating made-up scenarios in my head designed to make me feel like shit.

I slink to the back of the cafe and find the bathrooms right where he said they'd be. Classic silhouettes of a man and a woman decorate each door. I try the knob on the women's restroom and it turns with ease. I let out a tiny sigh of relief. I hate when the door is locked and I feel like I'm interrupting someone at a time when no one wants to be interrupted. It's even worse when they call out, "Someone's in here!" The awkward mortification I feel in those situations usually forces me to forgo using the bathroom. I can't risk waiting and coming face-to-face with the person who was inside. I've been known to hold my pee for hours in those situations. It's one of the reasons I've had so many bladder infections.

Once inside, I immediately notice how stark white and clean the bathroom is. It's a tiny one-stall room with a little white pedestal sink. There's a dark wooden table next to the sink with paper towels stacked in a neat tower. I grab one off the top and run it under the water. Giving my leg a few swipes, I clean off the grimy smear of dried street water. Lovely. With a new paper towel, I focus on my shoe. It's not as bad as I thought, thankfully, but there does seem to be a small water stain on the toe. I do the best I can with water and a little soap, and once I'm satisfied, I stroll back into the cafe. My fingers are crossed at my side as I exit the bathroom, hoping some customers have materialized since I've been gone.

They haven't.

The man behind the counter lifts his head when he hears my footsteps, even though I tried to move quietly. I've read about smiling eyes before, but I've never seen them. Until now.

"Found it okay?" he asks, though he doesn't need to.

"I did. Thank you."

He nods, still smiling. "You look like you could use a nice hot cup of coffee. Have a seat, and I'll fix you up." He tips his head toward the row of empty stools, and before I can decline his offer, his back is turned, and he's pulling a coffee cup down from a shelf.

I don't have time for coffee, but I don't feel like I can refuse it. Not after he let me use his bathroom. I walk to the counter and ease onto a stool. They're the kind that goes *pshhh* when you sit down. The orange pleather covers a spongy foam. Once I'm situated, I shift my body a bit to the left. Yep, it spins. I smile. I knew it would.

He places a little white saucer in front of me and glides a cup on top. It's filled three-quarters of the way with dark, amber liquid. The steam wafts up from the cup, and I inhale, collecting the magical aroma like it's manna from heaven. I love coffee.

"Let me get you some cream and sugar." He spins around and moves deftly behind the counter, collecting a porcelain bowl and a tiny pitcher. "There you are," he says, setting the bowl of sugar cubes and a small pitcher of cream in front of me. I've never had coffee served this way. So quaint and old-fashioned. I like it.

I deposit two cubes into my cup and enough cream to turn the color a light tan. Using the spoon he rested on the saucer he gave me, I stir the coffee a few times, tapping the spoon along the rim of the cup before setting it back on the saucer.

The man is busying himself on the other side of the counter but keeps glancing my way. I get the feeling he'd like to talk, but maybe he's afraid he'll bother me. Honestly, I'd welcome the conversation. Nothing bothers me quite like silence.

"So," I say, my voice slicing through the quiet like a knife. "I've never noticed this place before. How long has it been open?"

He eyes me curiously. "You must not come this way often."

I nod. "Not very, no."

"This place has been in my family for twenty years. My

grandfather first opened it as a five-and-dime, but over the years it's morphed as it's changed hands. It's been a cafe since I took over five years ago."

"Wow. I had no idea. So, Cole is—"

"My grandfather," he says, grinning. "And my dad. And also, me."

Now it's my turn to smile. "Truly a family affair, then."

He laughs. "Yes, you could say that."

I take a sip of my coffee. Simple and perfect. I close my eyes, savoring the taste. It's then that I notice the music. It's coming from somewhere off in the distance. There doesn't seem to be a speaker system in place, so wherever it is, it must be flowing out of a lone speaker somewhere. It's instrumental ambient type music with muted trumpets and a crooning man. It's haunting and old-fashioned and the perfect fit for this little cafe that time seems to have forgotten.

"This music," I say. "It's—"

"Distracting?" he offers.

"I was gonna say soothing, actually."

"Are you sure? Because I can turn it off. It's no problem." He moves toward the back left corner behind the counter. A small deco-style radio in a worn cherry wood finish is perched next to a rack of dishes.

"What is this place?" I mumble.

Cole rests a hand on top of the ancient radio. "Shall I change the station?"

"No, it's nice." He watches me. "Really," I add when it looks like he doesn't believe me.

He waltzes back toward me. "May I ask your name?"

Everything he says sounds so polite. So formal. It's oddly refreshing.

"You may." I smile. "It's Sylvia, but everyone calls me Sylvie."

"Well, Miss Sylvie, it's sure nice to meet you." He extends his hand, and I stare at it for a moment. "Go on. I won't bite, much." He winks.

We shake hands, and it's, well, strange. This whole interaction is unlike anything I've ever experienced.

Our moment is cut short when the door flies open, and a large, imposing man bursts in. "Give me a coffee, Cole. And while you're at it, how's about a piece of apple pie, too? And don't be stingy this time, you hear?" He waddles over, plopping onto a stool two seats down from me.

"Sure thing, Ollie," Cole says, letting go of my hand.

As he preps Ollie's coffee, it gives me a moment to collect myself, and I quickly remember—"Oh, shit, I'm gonna be late for work," I whisper under my breath.

"How much do I owe you?" I call out to Cole.

He glances up from the pie he's about to cut into. "It's on the house." He smiles widely.

"Are you sure?"

"I am."

"Hey," Ollie interrupts. "How come my coffee isn't free?"

Cole chuckles. "Because you're here every day, Ollie. You'd put me out of business."

"Fair," Ollie agrees.

"Well, thank you for the coffee and, um, letting me use your bathroom."

I'm just about to open the door when he says, "Anytime, Sylvie. Anytime."

With a tight-lipped smile, I nod, and then I leave.

CHAPTER TWO

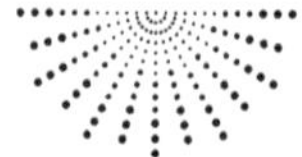

"*S*yl?"

"Hmm," I hum. The vibration in my throat reminding me of the low bass wafting out of that old radio in the coffee shop.

"Have you even been listening to a word I've said?" Melanie's voice is louder now, with an irritated pitch.

I blink a few times to clear the fog, but it's pointless. My body is here in the office, but my mind is back at Cole's Cafe, sipping warm coffee out of a porcelain cup.

"Sorry," I tell my friend. My only friend, who also happens to be my assistant. "I had a second cup of coffee this morning, and I'm beginning to feel the crash that comes after the energy burst." I stop short of telling her where I had that second cup. Cole's is a hidden gem, and I'm not sure I'm ready to share it just yet.

Melanie nods. She's a Starbucks junkie, so she's well-versed in the highs and lows of caffeine. "Anyway, as I was saying, you have a two o'clock with Allison to go over this month's numbers. I printed out a spreadsheet for you." She hands me a stapled packet of papers. "Oh, and there's an extra copy in there for her, too."

"Thanks, Mel. What would I do without you?"

"Fall flat on your face, of course," she says, not missing a beat and making us both laugh.

She sashays out of my office, closing the door with a gentle click. I'm left alone with my thoughts. Is it weird that they keep taking me back to Cole and his little cafe? It is weird, isn't it? I mean, I was only in there for half an hour. It's not like it was anything life-changing.

Still, there was something special about the place. It's a little out of my way, but I'm already planning on waking up a little earlier to stop in again.

A sharp knock on my door pulls me out of my reverie. I open my mouth to tell whomever it is to come in, but the door swings open before I have the chance.

Jackie waltzes in like we share the office. Breezing past my desk to stand in front of the window. I wait for her to say something, but she doesn't. Of course, she doesn't. This is the game she plays. The power move where she tries to make herself my superior. She's not. If anything, I rank above her if a ranking system existed here, which it doesn't. Not formally anyway. What we have is more of a status situation. Take our offices, for instance. Hers is down the hall and on the opposite side of mine. It's an interior walled-in room with no windows and is about half the size of my office. There's also a matter of how long we've been employed here at Dylan and Forsyth Design. This October will mark my fifth year working here, whereas Jackie is just shy of her second.

We don't have titles here. Allison Dylan doesn't believe in them. She says she finds them tasteless and limiting. But if I had one, it would be Chief Financial Officer, and if Jackie had one, it would be Senior Accountant. Both are important, but one is vital, and the other is, well, not as much.

"What can I do for you, Jackie?" I ask with a sigh.

"You meet with Allison today."

"I do."

"I thought I should take a look over the report to make sure the numbers are accurate." She stays facing the window like she can't be bothered to look at me. It's dismissive and really fucking irritating, as is her assumption that the numbers I've compiled are somehow wrong.

It takes everything in me to keep the annoyance out of my voice when I respond. "Thanks for the offer, but it's not necessary."

That gets her attention enough for her eyes to swing my way. They settle on my nose. I know this trick. I've used it myself. If you look at someone's nose, it gives the illusion that you're looking them in the eye. It's fairly effective, unless used on someone familiar with the tactic.

"Really, Sylvie. It's no problem. I'm already here. I may as well take a look." She strides over to my desk, spotting the report Melanie printed out. She reaches for the papers, but my reflexes are quicker, and I scoop them up before she has a chance.

"Really, Jackie," I mimic her words back at her. "I'm all set. Thanks."

I spin in my chair until I'm facing my computer. With my eyes locked on the screen, I begin typing away like this email is the most important one I've ever composed. Truthfully, I'm just typing gibberish in a draft, but Jackie doesn't know that. All she knows is I've dismissed her, and she's seething. I don't have to look at her face for confirmation. Her loud huffing and exaggerated footsteps, as she tromps toward my door, are proof enough. When she's about to leave, she hesitates.

"You know, Sylvie, it would be smart of you to take me up on my offer. It's always a good idea to have a second set of eyes look over an important report," she warns.

I give her my eyes for a moment just so I can watch my words land. "Oh, I have. Donna already took a look at it for me."

Jackie's darkened expression doesn't disappoint. She hates Donna, probably more than she hates me. They both started working here the same week, and Jackie has looked at Donna through a competitive lens ever since.

She grits her teeth and nods tersely before slinking out of my office.

I grin. I can't help it. I don't have a ton of things that make me happy here, but getting under Jackie's skin always does the trick.

"What was that all about?" Mel asks from the doorway. She is always ripe with office gossip because she never misses a thing. Just like she didn't miss this little interaction.

"Jackie was just being her usual helpful self," I say snidely.

"Ugh." Melanie rolls her eyes. "She's like a fucking Pitbull with a snake in its mouth."

"A what now?"

"Oh, you know," she says, flapping her hand. "Like how a Pitbull is always ready to pounce."

"I mean, I've heard people describe an eager person as a Pitbull, but the snake thing is new." I smirk.

"Yeah, well, that's because I added it. Because snakes are slimy and Pitbulls are eager and Jackie is both." She tips her head, proud of herself.

I chuckle. "Okay, I'll give you that one."

Melanie makes a dramatic display of checking the nonexistent watch on her wrist. "Speaking of eager, you should probably head over to Allison's office. You don't want to be late for your meeting."

I place a hand on my chest, affronted. "I would never."

She laughs. "You would and you have. Many times."

"Whatever," I say, shaking my head. I grab the report and

tap the page ends on my desk, straightening them. Sidling past Mel, I give her a wink. "Thanks again for these," I say, holding up the report.

She lifts a hand to her forehead, giving me a salute.

An hour later, Allison is smiling widely and complimenting me on a job well done. I smile and tell her how helpful Melanie was in putting the report together. The right words come out of my mouth, but my head is spinning. I just spent the entire meeting completely checked out. Kind of like how you can drive home and be shocked when you get there, having no memory of the drive, yet somehow you managed to make it there safely. Allison is walking me to the door and thanking me for my time, and all I can focus on is how easy it was for me to do my job like it's muscle memory. I'm not so sure that's a good thing.

"So? How'd it go?" Mel asks from behind her desk.

"All good," I say. "Your report was clean and perfect as usual, Mel."

She grins. "Glad to hear it."

The whole scene gives me déjà vu, but not in an *I've been here in another life* kind of way. More in a, *I've been here last month and the month before that and so on* kind of way.

I'm about to head back into my office when my eyes zero in on Mel as she sips from what's probably her third cup of coffee of the day. It gives me an idea.

"Hey, Mel? I think I might head out a little early today. I have a quick stop I want to make before I head home."

Her eyebrows raise. "Wait, Sylvie Masters is leaving early? Hold on. Let me get my camera to document this momentous occasion." She reaches into her purse and tugs out her phone.

I hold up my hands. "Will you stop? I've left early before."

She cocks her head. "Oh yeah? Name one time."

I think for a moment, then that moment becomes

minutes, and I've got nothing. I shrug. "Whatever. I'm your superior, so you can't question me."

She barks out a laugh that borders on hysteria. Within seconds she's swiping at her eyes, rubbing away tears. I roll my eyes and collect my things from my office. I stroll past my friend as she tries and fails to collect herself. I can still hear her laughing as the elevator doors close.

Let her laugh. I have better things to focus on right now. Like coffee. Coffee is what I need. And I know just the place.

CHAPTER THREE

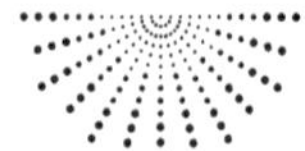

I woke up early this morning and told myself it was just a fluke. It wasn't planned. I didn't set an alarm. I just happened to open my eyes at 5:30 a.m. feeling refreshed. It has nothing to do with me wanting to stop in at the cafe on my way to work. And even less to do with the dreamy-eyed man behind the counter.

But as I stand here gripping the handle, my heart racing at the thought of the little bell chiming my arrival, Cole looking up from his spot with a grin, I know I'm a fucking liar.

I roll my eyes and open the door anyway. Foolishness be damned. After all, what's the harm in starting my day in the company of a nice person who just so happens to be easy on the eyes?

"Well, hello again, Miss Sylvie. Didn't expect to see you back so soon." Cole stands there with a smile more dazzling than I anticipated. And am I imagining it, or does he look genuinely happy to see me?

I'm projecting. And I need to stop it before I embarrass myself.

"Hi, Cole. You can just call me Sylvie. No need for such a proper greeting," I say with a smile as I meander toward the stools.

He frowns and it stops me in my tracks. Shit. Did I offend him?

"It's just, I only meant," I'm stammering like an idiot without any idea where I'm heading.

"It's okay, Sylvie," Cole says. "I was raised to always be respectful of women, but I was also raised to listen to them, too. And if you say I should drop the miss and call you by your first name, then that's what I'll do." He winks, and I practically melt.

Jesus, Sylvie. What's gotten into you?

I slide onto a stool and give myself a mental berating. I've been in the company of good-looking guys in the past, and I'm usually not so awkward. I wouldn't say I have game, necessarily, but I'd like to think I have enough self-confidence to know my worth.

Cole busies himself refilling the coffee pot, and I seize the opportunity to regroup. "So, I tried stopping by yesterday afternoon, but the door was locked." I cringe as I remember the disappointment I felt when I left work early, only to find the cafe closed.

"Must've been after two. We close at that time every day," Cole calls over his shoulder.

"Wow, lucky you. I'd love to end my workday at that time every day."

He spins around, holding a pot of coffee in one hand and a cup in the other. I think I liked it better when he wasn't looking at me. It was much easier to talk to his back.

"What's stopping you?" Cole sets the cup in front of me and fills it three-quarters of the way.

I cock my head. "What do you mean?"

"You said you wish you could end your workday at two.

Why don't you?"

I chuckle at his joke, but when he doesn't join in, I realize he might've been serious. And when he squints at me like he's having trouble seeing clearly, I know he wasn't kidding.

I sober up quickly. "That's just not how it works. I don't set my hours. The company does."

"Huh. Well, what if you owned the company? Then you could change things."

"Oh, that's not in the cards," I say, shaking my head.

"Why not?" he asks, pressing his palms on the counter.

I feel flustered. Not at the question, but because of his proximity. Well, maybe also at the question. I don't like to think about the future. Mostly because I set a goal for myself three years ago and I've achieved it. I don't know where else I can go from here. And if I think about that for too long, it scares me.

So, I take a sip of my coffee, stalling while I think of what to say. As the cup touches my lips, it dawns on me. I never asked Cole for coffee. He just knew I'd want some. Sure, it's early morning and coffee is a common drink at this hour, especially in a place like this. But it's more than that.

Cole knows how to read people. Not just because he knew I'd want coffee, but because he could see straight through the bullshit. He doesn't know me or what I do, but still, he was able to listen to my words and find a different meaning in them. One that I try to keep hidden. Especially from myself.

"So, you close at two. What time do you open?" I ask, shifting the attention back to him.

He grins in a way that tells me he knows what I'm doing, but thankfully, he plays along. "We open at six a.m. every weekday and at seven on Saturdays."

"And what about Sundays?"

"On Sundays we're closed." Coffee drips off the spout of

the pot Cole has sitting on the counter. He reaches for a rag and wipes it up.

"I'm guessing you must get a lot of the work crowd, huh? People stopping in to get their caffeine fix before starting their day." I glance around at the empty seats. "Is most of your business to-go orders?"

He gives me a blank look. "What kind of orders?"

"To go," I say a little more clearly. I have a tendency to mumble sometimes, especially when I'm nervous.

His expression doesn't change. He looks around, bewildered.

"I just mean, do people like to take their coffee with them after they've ordered it?" I feel as though I'm patronizing him, but he seems like he needs an explanation.

"Oh, as in ordering coffee, but not drinking it here?" He scrunches his face like the concept is foreign. I nod, and he continues, "No, no one has ever asked to take their coffee with them, but I suppose they could borrow a cup? If they were in a hurry and, of course, if it was someone I knew well enough to know they'd return the cup."

This exchange is so bizarre. It's hard to imagine anyone living in this century not understanding how to-go orders work. But then I look at the little pitcher of cream and the dish of sugar cubes and I realize, "You like to keep things old-fashioned, don't you?"

He flinches. It's only slight, but I clock it. Wow. I'm normally not this bad at small talk, but I am burying myself here. Superbly, I might add.

"Not old-fashioned," I rush to say. "Traditional."

He smiles, and I feel my whole body relax. "I find when something works, it's best to keep on workin' it."

I return the smile. "I can get behind that."

"Cole?" a woman calls as she bustles out from behind a swinging door. She's dressed formally in a royal blue dress with long sleeves. A white apron with lace trim covers her front. Her brown hair is swept up into a loose bun with silver tendrils framing her face.

"Oh," she says, stopping short. "Pardon me. I didn't realize you had a customer."

"It's all right, Mom. Come and meet Sylvie." Cole waves his arm toward me.

His mom's eyes do a quick sweep over me. Her cheeks seem to flush when she meets my gaze. "Pleased to meet you, Miss Sylvie." She doesn't come any closer, preferring to stay close to the kitchen door. It's as if she's leaving her options open in case she has to make a clean getaway.

"It's very nice to meet you, too, Miss, um, Mrs., uh." I glance at Cole for direction, but he just chuckles. I think my stammering amuses him.

"It's Carol, dear," his mom offers.

I give her a warm smile. "Ms. Carol," I repeat, settling on the title that doesn't assume her marital status.

"Sylvie here was just telling me she likes how I stick to tradition in the cafe." He smirks at Carol, and she rolls her eyes.

"Well, that's one word for it," she adds.

"Uh-oh, don't tell me I unknowingly contributed to a family argument."

They both laugh. "Not an argument, per se," Carol says. "It's more of a disagreement."

"Uh-huh," Cole agrees. "You see, my mom thinks I should start selling food at the cafe. Thinks it'll attract the lunch crowd. But Cole's Cafe has only ever served coffee, tea, and pie."

"Hmm," I muse. "And if something works, it's best to keep on workin' it, right?"

"Oh no, he's already gotten to you, hasn't he?" Carol frets, wringing her hands.

She seems genuinely concerned, and I immediately feel bad for making jokes. "I'm sorry. It's really none of my business, truthfully."

She tries to smile, but the corners of her mouth barely move. "It's just, the state of things isn't so great and, well, I just worry, is all."

Cole strides over and places a hand on his mom's shoulder. "It's okay, Mama. And if it's ever not okay, well, then we can talk more about your idea. All right?"

She grins, and this time her lips curve. "All right then, I'll leave you to it. Miss Sylvie, it was wonderful to meet you. I do hope you'll be back?" There's a lilt in her voice that conveys the same worry I heard when she was explaining herself to Cole a few moments ago.

I nod emphatically for her benefit. "Count on it."

With one last smile, she backs up and pushes her body against the door. It swings open for her and swings closed, hiding her from view.

"Your mom seems—"

"Sorry about—"

We both laugh. Cole gestures a hand toward me. "Ladies first."

"I was just gonna say your mom seems nice. It's wonderful that you get to work with your family."

Cole presses his lips together in a firm line. "Sometimes. Other times, I think I'm still viewed as the baby in the family. Never mind the fact that I've kept this place going over the past few years."

"I get it. It's nice to be recognized for the capable person you are and not someone they think is doing it all wrong."

"Uh-oh," Cole says. "Sounds like you might be speaking from experience."

I shrug. "A little. But mostly it's me who's my harshest critic."

"And why's that?" he asks, topping off my cup with more coffee.

I glance around the room and fix my gaze on the radio. The soothing sounds of soft trumpets and smooth clarinets act like a salve, quelling my anxiety. I don't like to talk about myself. If I admit my true thoughts, it feels like a weakness, and I didn't get where I am in life by being weak.

"I'm a goal-setter," I tell him. "Not in the impossible dream sense. I like to set attainable, albeit lofty goals for myself. And then it's a matter of not stopping until I achieve them."

He nods. "I can see that about you. You carry yourself well. You seem confident, but not boastful."

My face warms. "I am, for the most part. But see, the problem is, no matter how much I accomplish, I'm never fully satisfied." I look down at my hands in my lap. "I've never admitted that to anyone before."

Cole reaches across the Formica and rests a hand on my arm. "Hey," he whispers. I look up and find earnest eyes staring back at me. "Your secret is safe with me."

I know it is. That's why I spoke so freely. There's some-thing about this place, something about him, that makes me feel safe. And there's a part of me—a big part—that knows how crazy that sounds, but for now, I'm going to ignore it.

The little bell over the door chimes and a booming voice bellows, "I gotta clean the windows up on Windsor today, and you know those things are ancient. I swear I heard them cracking under my squeegee last time. So, listen, I'm gonna need a piece of your apple pie to get me through it. A big piece."

Cole chuckles. "Sure thing, Sam." He takes his hand away to get Sam's pie. The two of them fill the air with idle chitchat. I keep my eyes on my arm, to where my skin still tingles from Cole's hand.

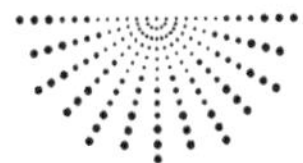

CHAPTER FOUR

"What kind of music is this?" Mel asks as she waltzes into my office, carrying a cup of coffee. She places it on my desk, wearing a face like she's smelling shit.

Old music heavy on the smooth trumpet flows out of the Bluetooth speaker on my bookshelf. "It's just some ambient playlist I found on Spotify. Why? You don't like it?"

"It's not that, it's just different from what you usually listen to. I mean, there's no lovesick emo boy singing with synthesizers harmonizing in the background." She smirks.

I ball up a Post-it note and toss it at her. She shifts her hip, dodging it and laughing.

"You can't even deny it, Syl."

I frown at her. "You love my eighties mix."

She rests a hand on her hip. "I wouldn't say I love it. I've just come to accept it."

"Whatever." I roll my eyes.

"So, what's the deal with this old-timey music, anyway?"

I crinkle my nose. "Old-timey?"

She tilts her head. "Sylvie, this is straight up the kind of music my grandparents listen to. In fact …" Mel's eyes widen, and she snaps her fingers. "This is their wedding song!"

"Ha. Ha. Ha," I say, dryly.

She laughs and swipes at a tear before it has a chance to trickle down her cheek and ruin her makeup. "No, really. What made you change up your music?"

"I don't know," I answer with a shrug. "I just felt like it was time to switch things up."

Except I do know. And my reason has dark brown hair and deep eyes, and he goes by the name Cole.

"Why are you smiling like that?" Mel squints at me, cocking her head.

I lift a hand to my mouth, and sure enough, I'm smiling like a damn idiot.

"Sylvia Masters. You've been holding out on me."

I place my palm on my chest, affronted. "What are you talking about?"

She stalks toward my desk and leers at me. "What's his name?"

"H-huh?"

"Sylvie," she warns. "Spill."

"It's not a guy," I lie.

"Well, it's something. You've got a tell, you know? Your right eyebrow always arches when you're hiding something. If it's not a guy, then what is it you're not telling me?"

I take a moment to get my thoughts in order, but Mel brings out the big guns.

"Come on, Sylvie. I thought we were best friends." She actually looks hurt, and now I feel awful.

How did this get so out of hand so fast? I'd love to tell her about Cole, but honestly, I feel foolish. I barely know him. He shouldn't have the effect on me that he clearly does.

But I have to tell her something. So, I say, "It's just this new coffee shop I recently discovered. It has this really old, er, traditional ambiance and they play music like this. It's just a vibe and I've been kind of into it." Also, the guy who runs the place isn't too shabby either. Of course, I leave that part out.

Mel looks intrigued. "A new coffee shop? Where's it located?"

"It's on Wellington. Right near the intersection at State."

"Huh." Her brows pull down. "I can't picture anything there."

"I know. I never saw it before, either. But Cole, the owner, told me it's been there for years. He inherited it from his grandfather."

Melanie nods but doesn't look convinced. "Hold on one second," she says before darting out of the room.

She's back a moment later with her phone in hand. Her fingers move rapidly on the screen. After a bit, she declares, "Uh-huh, just like I thought."

"What exactly is just like you thought?"

She flops her phone onto my desk. "There's nothing there except a row of abandoned buildings. They've been vacant for as long as I can remember."

I shake my head. She's obviously looking at the wrong spot. I pick up her phone and examine the screen. She's pulled up the location on Google Earth and switched it to street view. And she's right. The only things there are a few old brick buildings with windows broken out and graffiti on the exterior. I double check the coordinates, but she has them correct.

"Well, that's weird," I mumble.

"Is it possible you have the location wrong?" Mel asks.

I look off into the distance and retrace my steps. Within a few seconds, I'm pursing my lips and shaking my head. "Nope. That's where it is."

Mel picks up her phone, taking another look at the screen. "That's strange."

"Does Google ever make mistakes with things like this?"

She bites at her lip and nods slightly. "I mean, I don't think it's too common, but I guess it could be possible. Anyway, I know you have work to do so I'll leave you to it."

My mind is a million miles away, but I force a smile. "Thanks, Mel."

She smiles back, seeming satisfied. I wish I could say the same. When she reaches the door, she calls over her shoulder, "Oh, sorry if your coffee is a little on the sweet side. The sugar just sort of globbed out when I was pouring it."

I look down at the mug she placed on my desk. The steam wafting out of it when she first gave it to me has all but disappeared. It's probably lukewarm by now. Lifting the cup to my mouth, I take a sip, and yep, Mel was right. There's way too much sugar. It would be helpful if we had cubes here like Cole does. I know now that two lumps is the perfect amount.

"THIS IS FUCKING CRAZY," I mutter. Obviously, the cafe is here. I'm standing right in front of it. Still, I can't resist pulling out my phone and checking my location. A few taps later, I'm in street mode, and sure enough, it's showing an abandoned building where Cole's Cafe is.

Clearly, Google has made a mistake. Maybe somehow, pictures got crossed or something. The abandoned buildings are somewhere else, and probably wherever they are, it shows the cafe on street view. Somewhere, someone else is just as confused as I am, but for an entirely different reason.

Oh, well. Since I'm here, I may as well go inside. It would be rude if I didn't. I'm not sure how it would be rude, but I don't let myself dwell on it. It sounds convincing enough to make me feel better about coming here a third day in a row.

When I open the door, the bell chimes, and for the first time, I wish it hadn't. I don't know. I feel a little silly coming here so often. It would be nice to slip in unnoticed.

Cole isn't behind the counter. I don't see him anywhere, actually. And now, I'm considering leaving and reentering to see if he hears the bell a second time. Ugh. I'm a disaster.

A man sits at a round two-top in the corner. He's wearing a newsboy-style cap, and his nose is pressed deep into the paper. If he heard me come in, he doesn't seem to care. At least, not enough to acknowledge me.

I'm not sure what to do with myself, just standing here in the middle of the cafe. So, I tiptoe over to the counter and slide onto the same stool I've sat on the last two mornings.

The kitchen doors swing open a moment later, and Cole breezes out. He stops short when he sees me. "Sylvie, you're beginning to become a regular here, you know? Pretty soon, I'll be labeling that stool with your name on it." He winks.

I smile shyly. "What can I say? I seem to have developed a taste for traditional coffee in a porcelain mug."

He nods, looking away momentarily. When his gaze fixes back on mine, his eyes seem to shine. "Well then, I better get you that coffee." As he busies himself, he calls over his shoulder, "How's your morning been?"

"It's a morning," I say with a shrug, even though he can't see it.

He sets the cup on the counter and fills it. It's only been three days, but this is quickly becoming my favorite way to start the day. There's something about someone pouring a fresh cup of coffee for you. At home, it's just me, and it loses something when I'm the one holding the pot.

"Why do you say it like that?"

"Huh?" I blink a few times, looking up at Cole.

He presses his lips together. "You said 'it's a morning' like there's nothing special about it."

"Well, that's 'cause there really isn't. All of my mornings, afternoons, and evenings blend together. I can't really tell one apart from the other." Except that's not entirely true. Not anymore. These last three days have definitely been more memorable thanks to this cafe.

Cole frowns. "That's sad."

I lift a shoulder. "It's life."

"But it doesn't have to be."

I chuckle without humor. "Corporate America would disagree."

As I drop two lumps of sugar into my bowl, I remember what brought me here this morning. "Oh, I almost forgot. Your location is completely messed up on Google Maps."

"Goggle what?"

"Google," I say again. "You know, as in, they practically own the whole Internet."

He crosses his arms and pauses a moment. "This is where you work?"

"*Puh,*" I choke. "I wish. No, no, I work for Dylan and Forsyth Designs over on Greenwich. We're an interior design firm. Well, Dylan and Forsyth are. I don't have an artistic bone in my body. I'm more of a numbers girl." And I'm rambling.

Cole watches me with a strange expression on his face. It's a mix between amusement and curiosity.

"Hang on a sec," I say, reaching into my purse. "I'll pull up the site so you can see what I'm talking about."

The man at the corner table clears his throat, demanding Cole's attention.

"Sorry, Sylvie. Will you excuse me for a minute?"

"Sure thing," I say without looking up.

My phone opens with face ID, and I tap the browser app.

It opens a black screen with the words "no internet." I refresh the page, but the same message pops up.

"That's weird," I mutter. Then I notice the top right corner of my phone, where it usually shows the Wi-Fi or data status. But instead of "5G," it says, "SOS." I do the only thing I know how to do when technology isn't cooperating—I power it down. It reboots slowly, and after a few minutes, it's still not connecting. "Huh. I guess I must be in a dead zone."

"A what zone?" Cole asks, sidling up beside me.

Having him on this side of the counter throws me a bit off balance.

"Oh, um, just my phone. It can't seem to find a signal in here." I hold up the useless device and watch as Cole's eyebrows lift to his hairline.

"What did you say that was? A phone?"

First, he acted like he didn't know what Google was, and now he's behaving like he's never seen a smartphone before. He must be joking. And, okay, so his humor isn't as attractive as his face. That's actually good. It humanizes him.

I laugh, not because he's funny, but because I don't want to hurt his feelings. He doesn't laugh. He doesn't even smile. "Wait. You're not serious, are you? Surely, you know what a cell phone looks like."

"Sylvie," he says, taking long strides back to his position behind the counter. I'd miss his proximity if I weren't so confused right now. "This is a phone." He points to a black antique-style phone sitting on a table near the kitchen door. It's a rotary style with a handset and a cord.

"Wow, you really committed to the whole vintage thing, huh?"

He rubs his forehead. Something feels off. I can't put my finger on it. But when I feel uncomfortable, I've learned it helps to remove myself from the situation. Get a little distance.

So, I smile sweetly and say, "I'll be right back. I'm just gonna run to the bathroom."

He gives me a tight-lipped smile and a quick nod.

On my way to the bathroom, I walk past the table where the man had been sitting. He's gone, but he left the newspaper behind.

I don't know what compels me to do it, but I pick it up. It's a copy of the *New York Times*. There are pictures and articles all over the front page, but I don't see any of it.

My eyes are glued to the date printed under the masthead.

March 18, 1934.

CHAPTER FIVE

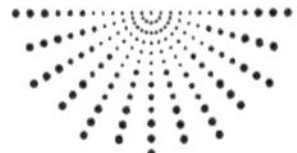

Holding the paper in my hand like it may disintegrate, I walk back to my stool. Cole's back is to me. He's wiping the counter in mindless circles.

"Cole?"

His hand stills, and he turns slowly to face me. "That was fast." The smile on his face is not the one I've come to expect from him. This one seems uneasy. Guarded.

I place the newspaper carefully on the counter in front of me. "I know this sort of goes with the theme in here, but do you think this should just be sitting out?"

"Where else would it be?"

"I don't know. Maybe behind a display case somewhere, protected from greasy fingers. I mean, a relic like this should really be preserved."

He chuckles. "A relic? Sylvie, it's just the newspaper."

I look away for a minute. This is strange. Somehow, things have gotten weird between us. It's like we're suddenly unable to communicate. It's as if we're speaking two different languages.

Still, I decide to try again and explain myself more clearly.

"You're right. It is a newspaper, but Cole, it's almost one hundred years old."

He rests a hand on the counter, leaning in. And when he speaks, his voice is low and soft. "It's not one hundred years old, Sylvie. This paper was printed this morning." He points to the date. "March 18, 1934, is today. What day do you think it is?"

Oh, no. No, no, no. I stand slowly and begin backing away. My head swivels, taking in the cafe with its vintage decor and the music with old-fashioned ambiance. And then I look at Cole as he stands there, looking back at me.

I suspect we're both wearing similar expressions, but only one of us has it right.

Cole hasn't just decorated his cafe like it's from another century. He actually believes it is.

I feel sad for him and pity for me. I thought I had found a new friend or maybe more. That's what I get for letting my emotions take the helm. I've been so preoccupied with batting my eyes at the beautiful man behind the counter, I failed to see that he's not well.

But I see it now. And I hate myself for thinking this, but I wish I hadn't. I wish I could go back to fifteen minutes ago before things between us started to shift. I could've just kept coming in here for coffee and conversation. Which, more than likely, would've still ended up exactly where we are right now.

My feet keep moving backward, taking me to the door. Cole doesn't speak. And neither do I. What more could we say? We both think the other is horribly confused.

I'm outside a moment later, standing in the middle of a busy sidewalk. People race around me in hurried clumps, too preoccupied with getting to work on time to notice the sad girl on the pavement.

This is just my luck. I finally find something that brings a tiny spark to my day. A little bit of light amidst all the gray. And that quick, it's gone.

I scrub a hand down my face and cast my gaze to the sky. It's overcast and gray, just like my life.

A drop of water lands on my forehead, followed by one on my cheek. They're quickly joined by more, and then it's pouring.

Perfect.

I WIGGLE my key in the lock while simultaneously twisting the knob. I've complained about this faulty lock for months, and Jerry, my well-meaning yet do nothing, landlord, has yet to have it repaired.

After a few more vigorous jostles—some may be a bit more violent than necessary—the door finally pops open, and I trip into my apartment. My shoes squelch on the floor, and water drips from my sopping clothes.

I shove the door closed and lock it behind me. Then I strip down to my underwear right in the entryway. I tiptoe toward my bedroom, stopping first at the laundry closet to deposit my wet clothes into the dryer.

In my room, I slip on an oversized sweatshirt and tug on some leggings. They stick to my wet legs, which is super fun. As I'm jumping up and down, pulling on the waistband, I notice the clock on my nightstand.

"Shiiit!"

It's after nine. I should've been at work a half hour ago. It's so late, and I'm never late. Well, never this late, anyway. Mel is probably freaking out right about now.

I rush back to the foyer, where I dropped my purse on the floor, and when I finally dig out my phone, there are four missed calls from Mel and eight texts. I'm just about to call her when my phone rings.

"Hey, Mel."

"Sylvie? Are you okay? Are you lying in a ditch somewhere? Should I call an ambulance?"

"Okay, deep breaths, Mel. Come on, do it with me. In through the nose and out through the mouth." I breathe into the phone, encouraging her to do the same.

"Okay, fine," she huffs. "I'm calm. Now will you tell me why you're not at work?"

"Well, I was on my way and …" I pause, unsure of how to word things. I don't want to tell Mel about Cole. It doesn't feel right. "And, um, I just started feeling off and then the rain came and I got soaked. So, I came home and that's where I am right now."

"You're sick? Huh. In all the time I've known you, I don't think you've ever taken a sick day."

"I haven't."

"Well," she says. "I think it's great."

"What?" My face scrunches.

"Not that you're sick. Just that you're putting yourself first, for once."

I nod, but I'm not so sure she's right. It feels more like I'm hiding.

We hang up, and I look around my apartment. It's furnished with the necessities, but it still feels empty. Cole may be extremely confused when it comes to what decade we're living in, but he was right about one thing. This life I'm living is pretty sad.

CHAPTER SIX

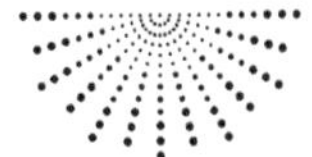

I can't believe I'm actually back here. I've avoided this place for a week after learning the owner thinks it's 1934. But I've been thinking a lot about what happened—trying to come up with logical reasons for thinking so illogically.

Suppose Cole has a form of amnesia. I mean, it could happen, right? Maybe he has a brain injury that's made him confused.

Or maybe he's just into pretending. Kind of like a cosplay thing. Sure, it may seem a little weird, but those people who dress up for conventions seem happy. Who's to say Cole isn't seeking that same level of happiness and he's just really immersed himself?

No matter the reason, the truth is, I miss coming here. Which is odd since the few times I was here add up to a mere blip in my life. But it was a really pleasant blip.

And I miss it. The coffee and the company, but mostly I miss that feeling of having something to look forward to.

Cole is wiping down the counter and pauses mid-swipe

when he hears the bell chime. His eyes widen as he takes me in.

"Sylvie. I didn't think you'd be back."

"Neither did I."

"How've you been?"

I shrug. "Okay. How about you?"

"The same." The corner of his mouth lifts. It's not the wide smile he normally wears, but it still feels welcoming.

And it's the push I need. I've been standing by the door, unable to move any closer, but now I stroll over to my stool.

As I sit, Cole says, "No one's sat there since you were last here."

"Are you serious?"

He nods. "I told you, you're a regular. Or, at least you were."

"Am," I say, smiling.

His body relaxes a bit. "Let me get you your coffee."

As I sip, he tells me about his mom's blueberry pie and how she can't seem to make it fast enough. I tell him I'd like to try a piece. He asks about work. I say it's work. He chuckles.

The conversation is easy, but that's because we're avoiding the gigantic century-old elephant in the room. I'm not planning on bringing it up, and it looks like neither is he.

"This pie is amazing. I can see why it's selling out so quickly," I say between bites.

Cole grins proudly. "My mom is really an amazing baker."

"It must've been pretty great growing up in a house with a mom who could bake like this." I hover the fork over my plate and use it to point at the pie.

A wistful expression settles on his face. "It was. Some of my favorite memories as a child happened around our dinner table."

"Are you an only child, or do you have any siblings?"

"I have two brothers. Both younger than me. One works at a bank about an hour from here and the other just joined the army." He rubs at his eyebrow.

"That worries you."

"What does?"

"Your brother who joined the army."

He lets out a puff of air. "Well, if you knew John, you'd understand why I'm worried."

"Tell me about him."

"I don't even know where to begin." He laughs. "John was the kind of kid you never needed to dare twice. In fact, you'd barely need to dare him at all. He was just always doing crazy things." He gets a faraway look in his eye. "There was this one time when I was about ten and John was seven. We were out walking on the train tracks near our house and we felt them start to rumble. I got off right away and started walking a safe distance from them, but not Johnny. No, he just kept walking on those damn tracks. I told him to move, but he said he wanted to dodge the train."

I lean in, resting my chin on my hand. "What happened?"

"The asshole dodged it," he says, shaking his head.

"So, you're afraid he'll put himself in danger if the opportunity arises."

"I'm afraid he may encounter a train he can't dodge."

His words are heavy with innuendo. I can't blame him. John sounds reckless.

"What about you?" Cole asks.

"What about me?"

"Do you have any brothers or sisters?"

I shake my head. "No. I'm an only child."

"One of those, huh?" He grins.

"Yep," I say, popping the *p*.

"How about your parents?

"Um, they don't live around here." There's a tiny black

smudge on the counter in front of me, and I stare at it like it's the most fascinating thing I've ever seen.

Cole clears the plate in front of me, walking it over to a large sink behind him. He rinses it with water before setting it inside.

"Please tell your mom how much I enjoyed the pie."

He smiles. "I will."

There's a pause, and I'm hopeful he won't ask me any more questions about my family. But my hope is quickly dashed when he speaks again.

"You said your parents don't live around here. Do you get to see them often?"

I hate conversations like this, and I only have myself to blame. I started it by asking Cole about his family. Of course, he would return the favor.

I'm stuck in my head, thinking of what to say, when Cole interrupts my thoughts. "It's okay. You don't have to tell me if you don't want to."

"It's not that I don't want to."

He cocks his head, studying me in that way that he does. The one that lets me know he's on to me.

"Okay, fine. I don't want to, but not because I have anything to hide. I'm not embarrassed about them. They're decent people. They're just very … distant."

"Distant," he echoes.

"Yeah. They've never been the type of parents who are super interested in their child's life. Honestly, I think if they could do it all over again, they'd never have had me."

He shakes his head. "No, I'm sure they would."

"You'd think so, wouldn't you? I mean, after all, how could parents wish their child had never been born? But trust me. Mine do."

"Why do you think they don't love you?" he asks. His voice is soft and calm.

"Oh, they love me. I just don't think they like me very much, is all."

He frowns, looking pained. I know this expression. It's the same one Mel wore when I told her this story. And it's one I won't tolerate. I don't want to be pitied.

"Listen. Don't feel sorry for me. My parents were young when I was born. They weren't even married, but everyone insisted they fix that. So, you see, I wasn't planned and, in fact, I reframed their entire lives. Why wouldn't they want a do-over?"

"That wasn't your fault. You didn't ask to be born."

"No, you're right. I didn't. But I was." I lift a shoulder. "It's okay. I've made peace with it. I just don't really like to dwell on it, you know?"

He presses his lips together and nods. "I understand."

Amicable silence settles over us. He remains behind the counter, a thoughtful look dancing in his eyes. I sip my coffee, feeling glad I took a chance and came back here.

Human interaction is something I think we often take for granted. Sure, I talk to people at work every day, but never with any real depth. Aside from Mel, I don't talk about myself to anyone. Not even me. I barely let myself think about my life. Because if I do, I always overanalyze it.

I'm twenty-seven.

I should be married by now.

I should own a home.

I should have kids.

I should have people of my own.

People who genuinely care about me.

I shouldn't be alone.

Those are dark thoughts, and nothing good ever comes of them.

A short, balding man with wire-rimmed glasses comes

bursting through the door. The poor bell barely has time to react and makes more of a clanking sound than a chime.

"Cole! There you are!" he shouts.

Cole stands at attention. His eyes narrow, and his jaw works back and forth. "Where else would I be, Dan?"

Dan laughs. It's rough and scratchy. "Ah, you kill me. Always the joker, this one." He says that last line to me. His beady eyes flare and begin to move all over me, pausing in places they have no business pausing.

Cole clears his throat and it's practically a growl. "What can I do for you?"

Dan redirects his attention away from me, and I feel instant relief.

"Listen, pal, I was just wondering if you gave any more thought to that little business venture I talked to you about." He leans in, pressing his meaty palms on the counter entirely too close to mine. I pull back, resting my hands on my thighs.

Cole shakes his head and rolls his eyes. "Dan, I've told you over and over. The answer is no. And it won't change."

"Ah, sure it will. You just aren't thinking clearly, so allow me to help. See, you revamp this joint, maybe darken the walls, add some low lighting and change this counter into a cherry wood bar top. Then you trade in your coffee on booze and trust me, the money will come pouring in." He chuckles at his idiotic pun.

Cole looks bored, standing there with his arms crossed. He's leaning back on the counter behind him. On a sigh, he lifts his gaze to the ceiling before settling it back on Dan with a sear so pointed, I swear it could draw blood. "I'm going to speak really slow for you because I get the sense that you're a man who only hears what he wants. I am never going to turn my cafe into a bar. Not now. Not ever."

Dan tsks, and tiny droplets of spit fly from his mouth. One lands on my nose, and my weak gag reflex kicks in. I start coughing. Cole jumps into action, filling up a glass of water and placing it in front of me.

Dan behaves as though I'm not hacking up a lung beside him. He scrubs a hand down his face like he's trying to reset his emotions, and when he speaks, it's as though he's talking to an old friend. I don't know the history between him and Cole, but judging by this interaction alone, they aren't friends. At least, not according to Cole.

"Buddy," Dan drolls. "The end of prohibition is still a hot topic. It's only been a year. You should jump on the train and rake in the dough."

Prohibition? What is he talking about?

"Okay, Dan, well, thanks for stopping by." Cole spins around and straightens coffee cups that don't need straightening.

Sensing he's been dismissed, Dan turns to me. "See if you can get through to your boyfriend here. Maybe he'll listen to you."

I open my mouth to say … so many things. He's not my boyfriend. I'm not going to convince him to do anything. What the hell do you mean by "the end of prohibition is still a hot topic"? But I say none of those things because Dan slinks out of the cafe like the snake he is.

And I'm left wondering.

"Was that a setup?"

Cole spins around with an eyebrow raised. "Pardon?"

"That guy," I say, arcing my thumb toward the door. "Did you hire him?"

"Hire him? Why would I do that?" Cole pulls in his lips and presses them together. He looks uncomfortable, and I think maybe I caught him.

"So you can continue with this narrative that it's 1934 and not 2023, that's why." I cross my arms and give him a look that says, "Check mate."

He doesn't react the way I expect him to. The smile on his face is sad. He shoves his hands deep into his pockets and looks down at the black shoes on his feet. When he finally lifts his head, he looks utterly defeated.

"Sylvie, it *is* 1934."

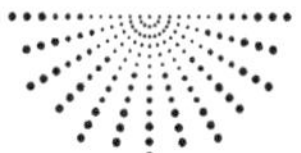

CHAPTER SEVEN

"Not this again." I sigh, running a hand through my long brown hair. "I was hoping we could just pretend that never happened."

"Pretend?" Cole asks, his voice lifting. "Sylvie, you think it's the year 2023. How can I pretend that's not a problem?"

I shake my head. "I don't *think* it is. I *know* it is. You're the one who thinks it's a different year." I feel my heart pick up slightly, the way it always does when my irritation begins to rise.

"It IS 1934! You saw the paper! You heard Dan talk about prohibition. Sylvie, that ended last year."

"The newspaper proves nothing, and Dan proves even less. The year is 2023. I was born on a brisk January morning. It was the tenth and the year was 1995. I wasn't even alive in 1934." I roll my eyes. "And neither were you, I might add."

Cole scratches the top of his head. "Are you always this incorrigible?"

"Are you?" I challenge.

"What will it take to get you to understand?"

"That I've time traveled?" I ask.

"That you're confused," he says softly.

I close my eyes and focus on my breathing for a moment. This situation is obviously beyond my capabilities. My degree is in accounting, not psychology. Poor Cole. He needs help, and I don't think I'm the right person to give it to him.

But I have an idea …

"Humor me for a moment, would you? Come outside with me. I can show you really quickly what year it is."

"Why would outside be any different?"

"Because," I say, rising out of my seat. "My phone works out there. It's all the proof you'll need."

He watches me with a careful eye as he makes his way out from behind the counter. Without thinking too deeply, I extend a hand toward him, and he takes it, threading his fingers with mine. I don't let myself dwell on how good it feels. I'm doing this to prove a point and nothing more. Once I'm done, Cole will realize he needs to see someone. Someone more qualified to help him.

We walk with tentative steps toward the door. I rest a hand on the knob and look back at Cole. "On the count of three. One."

"Two," he says.

"Three." I twist the knob as I say the word and push out onto the sidewalk.

But something happens. He lets go of my hand just as I step outside. This is worse than I thought. He's not willing to accept the truth.

With a sigh, I go back into the cafe. I don't see Cole anywhere. I call his name, but there's no answer.

A few minutes later, he comes back in through the same door I just entered. When he sees me, he stops, crosses his arms, and tilts his head.

We speak at the same time.

"Why didn't you come outside?"

"Where were you?"

"I was outside looking for you," Cole answers. "But you were still in here." The corners of his mouth turn down.

I shake my head. "I wasn't in here. I was out there." I point at the door. "But I didn't see you. You let go of my hand."

"I didn't let go of your hand. You let go of mine."

My skin erupts in goosebumps and feels like it's crawling with bugs. He doesn't sound like he's lying, but neither am I. And how can that be? I didn't let go of his hand, and he's saying he didn't let go of mine. My brain can't make sense of any of this.

"I have another idea," he says, walking toward me. He picks up my hand that's lying limp at my slide and tugs me toward the kitchen door. He pushes inside and heads straight for the closed door in the back. When he reaches it, he turns to me. "No counting this time. Just hold on to my hand and don't let go." And with that, he shoves the door open.

We step outside, but no outside I've ever seen. Antique cars drive by on a narrow road. The sidewalk isn't as filled with people as I'm used to, but the people I do see look different. The men wear suspenders and long coats. Some wear wide-brimmed hats, while others have on newsboy caps like the man from the cafe.

There are more men than women, but I do see a few with their arms threaded through a man's arm. They wear dresses —every single one of them. The dresses look like they might be something you'd wear to a party, and they're all long, practically touching the ground.

I crane my neck to look down the street. I notice tracks in the road, and a moment later, a streetcar comes careening past us.

"Does this look like 2023?" Cole whispers in my ear. His

warm breath skates across my neck, sending shivers over my shoulders.

I look at him with wide eyes and a wider mouth. I've been speechless before, but this is like all the words in the entire universe have suddenly become unusable.

He must sense how overwhelmed I am because he's quickly tugging me back inside the cafe. We stand close together in the kitchen, both of us breathing audibly. He thinks he's made a breakthrough, but in actuality, he's complicated things beyond comprehension.

"Cole," I whisper. "I don't understand what's happening."

"I know, but it's okay. You just need some help."

I look at him with unblinking eyes. "I don't doubt that, but not for the reason you think."

He frowns. "For what reason then?"

"Because in here and out there," I say, pointing to the door we just came through, "it's 1934. But out there?" I gesture toward the front door. "It's 2023."

"Sylvie—"

"No, listen, please. I'm completely serious. I'm from the future. Jesus," I mutter. "Yeah, I know how crazy that sounds, but it's true."

He looks at the floor and then the wall. He's avoiding me, and I don't blame him. I don't know how to make him believe me.

My purse hangs off my arm. I reach in and retrieve my phone. It powers on, and I glance at Cole to find him watching me. "It unlocks using my face for identification. See?" I hold up my phone, and it opens once it registers my face.

Cole's eyes widen. I swipe my fingers across the screen, showing him the apps I've downloaded. "This one is a to-do list. It helps me stay organized. And this one? It's for listening to podcasts." His face scrunches. "Those are kind of like talk radio shows."

He nods, and his throat bobs with a hard swallow. "I'm afraid I'm at a loss for words."

"I know the feeling," I tell him. "But looking at this phone, you can't deny what I'm saying. There's no technology in 1934 capable of creating something like this."

"And out there," he says, tipping his head toward the door we just came in from, "there's no denying what year it is. I don't know much about what the future holds, but I'm certain it'll look very different from the 1930s."

"You're right about that."

"So, what now?" Cole asks.

"Hell if I know." I look back at my phone and notice the time. "For the time being, we'll have to table this discussion. I need to get to work."

"Work at a design firm in 2023."

I nod. "And you need to get back to work in a cafe in 1934."

He lets out a puff of air. "There's one thing we have in common."

"What's that?" I ask.

"Neither one of us is going to be able to concentrate much today."

I chuckle and so does he. It feels odd to laugh at a moment like this, but it also feels like the only logical response.

"Um, well, I guess I'll see you later?" I say, feeling shy all of a sudden.

He raises his eyebrow. "That's up to you."

"I guess it is." I give him a small wave and make my way toward the exit. Or should I call it a portal? God, this is fucking weird.

Cole follows silently behind me. As I reach the door, he

calls out, "Be careful out there. Don't get hit by any flying cars."

I snicker. It's funny how we all assume the future brings flying transportation. I'm still waiting on hoverboards that actually hover.

"See you soon," I say, and then I'm back in the present day.

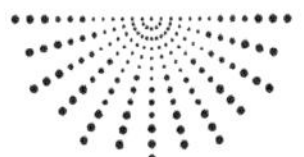

CHAPTER EIGHT

The cursor on my screen blinks, and I know it's mocking me. Come on, Sylvie, do your thing. Type your numbers. Input your data. It should be easy to do the same thing I do every single day. But today, my mind is stuck in the past. In the year 1934, to be exact.

Did all of that really happen this morning? Now that there's some distance between things, I'm starting to doubt it all.

As I stare at the screen, I realize something. I could easily look the cafe up online. If it exists now, I'll know I've imagined all of this. That should scare me. If I've created this scenario in my head, I'm obviously going to need to confront that, but somehow the idea that I've hallucinated still brings me more comfort than thinking I can time travel.

I type Cole's Cafe Wellington Avenue into the search box. My finger hovers over the mouse button. All it takes is one click to find answers. But do I want them?

Yeah, I think I do. Otherwise, I'm going to be stuck in this weird limbo. If the search yields results, it'll give me peace of mind, or it'll royally fuck me up. Either way, I'll know what I'm up against.

Just as I click the button, Melanie walks in. "Knock, knock," she says, not knocking.

"Hey, Mel." It takes everything in me to look away from the screen.

"Hey, yourself. I didn't see you come in this morning. You got here early. You aren't still trying to make up for taking that sick day last week, are you? That's not a requirement, you know?" She rests her hands on her hips, and from the way she's looking at me, it feels like I'm back in elementary school getting a stern talking to by my teacher.

"I do know that, but thanks for the reminder." I give her a cheeky smile.

"Good," she says, nodding like she's proud of herself. "I just popped in to give you a heads-up."

"Oh no, what about?"

She waves her hands. "No, it's nothing bad. And definitely not Jackie related."

"Thank God for small favors."

She chuckles. "How about it? Every day without an interaction with her is a good day."

"You can say that again." Mel opens her mouth to do just that, but I hold up my hand. "Only a figure of speech, Mel."

"Oh, you're no fun." She scoffs.

"You're just figuring that out?"

She rolls her eyes, ignoring my self-deprecating comment. "Allison sent me an email requesting to get on your calendar. Apparently, there's a new strip mall going in nearby and we've been contracted to do some design work at an orthodontist's office."

"Another strip mall?" I whine.

"Oh, you shush your mouth! This one's gonna have a Trader Joe's!" Mel squeals, jumping up and down.

I laugh. "Fine. I guess that's acceptable."

"Anyway," she continues, "Allison says she needs some advice on budgeting for this one. You'll be meeting with her tomorrow morning at ten for some good old-fashioned number crunching. Sounds fun." She says that last part dryly, lifting her eyes to the ceiling.

I heard what she said, but I'm stuck on two words in particular. *Old-fashioned*. Just like Cole's Cafe. Except in there, it's not old-fashioned; it's present day. Or maybe …

My eyes drift back to my computer screen, but Mel clears her throat, reminding me she's still here.

"Um, sure, that should be just fine." I try pretending like I was thinking things over and hope it worked.

"You okay?" Mel asks.

She knows me too well.

"Yeah, I'm just a little tired, is all."

"Hold on. Are you telling me Sylvia Masters, reigning champion of workaholics, is actually admitting—out loud—to being tired?" She throws her hands up over her mouth in mock horror.

"I *am* human, you know."

"You sure about that?"

"You're quite the comedian," I deadpan.

She pats her hair. "I am, aren't I? Well, my fellow human, you're lucky you have me. Apparently, I'm in high demand."

"I'm totally lucky, but what do you mean? Did something happen?" I lean forward, resting my elbows on my desk.

"Oh, it's nothing, I'm sure. Just some head hunter—in New York City, of all places—sent me an email about some executive assistant position at a law firm or something like that."

"That's exciting. Are you gonna look into it?" I'd hate to lose Mel, but I also never want to be the one to hold her back.

She shakes her head dismissively. "Like I'd ever leave you."

"Mel, come on. You know I love you, but you don't need to stay here for me. This place is fine, but you might want to explore all of your options. Think about it. You could be working in some high-rise in NYC while the rest of us are stuck working on strip mall budgets." I waggle my eyebrows.

"Pssh, if I left, I'd miss all the fun." She laughs. "I'm afraid you're stuck with me. I'll let you get back to work." She taps on my desk before whisking out of my office.

As soon as the door closes, my eyes zing back to my waiting Internet search.

I scan the results, and when I reach the third one, my eyes practically bulge out of my head.

Beloved cafe closes its doors after fifty years.

I can see a bit of the article where it mentions Cole and the cafe by name, but I can't bring myself to click on it. I don't know what it is, but it just feels wrong. Like it's information I'm not supposed to know.

One thing is certain, though. Cole's Cafe did exist, but in the year 2023, it no longer does.

I close out the browser and push out of my chair. I need a change of scenery.

I leave my office and meander down the hall, waving at Pat working feverishly behind his desk. I pass Kathleen on my way into the break room.

She smiles. "Hi, Sylvie."

"Hi-ya, Kathleen."

She props a hand against her mouth like she's about to tell me a secret. "There's one more Twix in the vending machine, and it has your name on it," she whispers.

I grin mischievously and rub my hands together. "Ooh, come to mama."

We chuckle and wave as I breeze into the room.

Kathleen was right. There's one more Twix left, and it's exactly what I need. Inserting my dollar into the machine, I'm about to press the buttons when a shrill voice sounds from behind me.

"Time for a sugar fix, huh?"

Jackie.

"Hi, Jackie." I try and fail to sound happy to see her.

"I'd be careful if I were you," she says, sidling up beside me. "All those extra calories are gonna catch up to you one day."

I press the buttons on the machine a little harder than necessary. The corkscrew of metal spins, releasing my Twix to the bottom. I retrieve it and make a show of opening it in front of her. Without uttering another word, I take a bite of one of the bars, closing my eyes to accentuate how good it tastes. When I open them, she's staring at me with her mouth agape.

I stroll out of the room, stopping at the door and calling back to her, "I'd be careful if I were you. You keep your mouth open much longer and flies are gonna start swarming." And then I'm gone with a wicked grin plastered on my face.

"What's got you smiling like that?" Mel asks as I come into view.

"Just had a little run-in with Jackie and I managed to leave her speechless."

Mel claps and whistles. "Good. Now keep the momentum going. Hopefully, it'll help you get through the phone call that's waiting for you."

"Phone call?"

Mel grimaces. "Your aunt is on line two."

I sigh. "Fantastic."

I set my candy on my desk. I'm definitely going to need it after I'm done with this call.

Lacing my fingers, I push my hands in front of me, palm side out, cracking a few knuckles. I let out a puff of air and then pick up the handset.

"Here goes nothing," I mutter, pressing the button.

Plastering a smile on my face that I hope she can hear, I croon into the phone, "Aunt Bethany. What can I do for you?"

"Sylvia? Is that you?"

Never mind that she called me and I answered by saying her name. Either of those should've tipped her off, but this is how she is. So, I grit my teeth and say, "Uh-huh. How are you?"

"Oh, dear, well, I'm afraid I'm not good at all."

Of course, she isn't. Aunt Bethany is my mother's sister and the only member of my family who ever voluntarily tries to contact me. But that's only because I made the mistake of loaning her money for a down payment on a car a few years ago. Now she calls me every so often with another "woe is me" story.

"What's the matter, Aunt Bethany?"

"That damn Roger lost his job again." Roger is my uncle, and according to Bethany, he's a "lazy piece of shit." Of course, Aunt Bethany's never worked a day in her life, so it's a little bit of pot meet kettle.

"I'm sorry to hear that," I lie. "What happened?"

"Oh, who the hell even knows? My guess is he mouthed off to someone. Anyway, it's not important. The problem is, I ordered a new sofa and the furniture people won't deliver it until I pay the balance and with Roger out of work ..."

I feel every bit of that ellipsis. She's waiting for me to fill in the blank with the words I always say. I could say no, but the truth is, I have more money than I need and no one to share it with. This is what desperation looks like.

"No worries. I'll transfer money to you. How much do you need?"

"Sylvie girl, you are a lifesaver! What would we do without you?" Probably pay for your own shit. "I don't need much. Seven hundred and fifty dollars should do it."

"Okay, I'll send it right over—"

"Give me a minute, will ya?" Bethany yells to someone. A second later, she's speaking into the phone. "Sylvie, I need to dash. Your uncle made a mess in the kitchen again. I swear that damn man is going to send me to an early grave! Thanks again, dear. Talk soon." *Click.*

I groan and place the phone back in its cradle. Pulling up my bank app on my phone, I tap a few things and send the money off to my aunt.

"How much did she ask for this time?" Mel asks, leaning against the doorframe.

"Seven hundred and fifty dollars. Not as much as last time." I say that like it's a good thing.

"I don't know why you insist on giving her money every time she asks. What are you getting out of this relationship besides a headache?" She arcs a brow.

I run a hand through my hair. "She's family," I say with a shrug.

"Oh, Sylvie. You're too good for your own good, you know that?"

"I don't even know what that means."

"Of course, you don't," she sighs. "Of course, you don't."

CHAPTER NINE

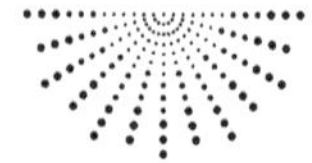

"Well, well, how's future girl this fine morning?" Cole smirks.

"So, we've already advanced to joking about this?"

He shrugs. "It seems like the only logical option."

"I suppose," I say, strolling up to the counter.

Cole reaches for a coffee cup and has it in front of me before my bottom touches the stool. He fills it and slides the cream and bowl of sugar cubes onto the counter.

I prepare my coffee under his watchful eye, and just as I'm about to take my first sip, I pause. "You never let me pay for anything in here, but I have to ask. How much do you charge for a cup of coffee?" I carefully nurse the hot drink, savoring the rich, nutty flavor. Cole makes the best coffee.

"Twenty-five cents," he says proudly.

I sputter, and a spray of coffee flies from my mouth. Cole rushes to get a napkin and quickly holds it out to me. I dab at my face while he wipes up the counter.

Once I have my fit under control, I practically shout, "Twenty-five cents? You're joking!"

He squints at me and shakes his head. "I'm not. We just raised it, in fact. A month ago, it was twenty cents."

I press a hand over my mouth, scoffing. I shouldn't be surprised. I am currently one hundred years in the past, but it's so hard to wrap my head around how different things were. When I'm in here alone with Cole, I can't tell I'm in the past, and I don't think he can tell I'm from the future either. We're just two people who like each other's company. But then something like this happens, and I remember how different we are.

"Can I ask how much you pay for coffee where, uh, you're from?" He stumbles over his words, and it's adorable. I'm from the same place he is, just a different time. But I know what he means all the same.

"Well, that depends."

"On?" he goads.

"What exactly it is you want to order and then what size you're ordering, too."

"So complicated," he says, shaking his head. "Why don't you just tell me how much it usually is for whatever you order."

I think on it for a moment, finally settling on my favorite drink from Starbucks. "I usually get a grande white chocolate mocha and that's around six dollars or so."

Now it's Cole's turn to sputter. "That's insane. Is everyone in the future rich? Or maybe you're all broke if you're paying that much for coffee."

"We're definitely not all rich or poor, for that matter. Where I'm from, the value of a dollar is different than it is here."

Cole nods. "That's for sure. I'm lucky if I bring in six dollars during the morning rush, and that's only on a good day. Haven't had as many of those lately." He mumbles that last part, but I still heard it.

"Why haven't your days been good?" I'm offended, and that's ridiculous. He's not talking about me, but a part of me worries he might be. I've been coming in here a lot. Maybe too much. I'm a distraction.

"It's not my days that have been bad. As a matter of fact, they've been some of the best I've had in a long time." He smiles, letting me know those words were for me. "What I meant was things have been a little slow lately as far as business goes. Slower than I'd like. Slower than I'm used to."

I press my lips together and nod solemnly. I don't remember much from history class, but I know Cole is currently living through the Great Depression. I'm actually surprised the effect hasn't been as devastating on his business as it has for others.

It makes me wonder. "How've you managed this far?" I'm careful not to bring up the recession by name, and it dawns on me I have knowledge of what's to come for him. Kind of like a fortune teller.

"I have my regulars and, to be honest, my grandfather was a shrewd businessman. He made some investments and left me with a successful business and money to spare."

"That's really great. Your grandfather sounds pretty amazing."

"He was," Cole says with a lopsided smile.

"So, since I come from the future, I know things. I could give you some insight if—"

"No," he snaps.

I wince. "O-okay, I was just trying to help."

His expression softens. "I know you were. I'm sorry. I didn't mean to bite your head off. I just ..." He trails off, running a hand through his hair. It ripples between his fingers like waves in a choppy ocean. "I don't think we should mess with things in that way. It feels dangerous for you to tell me things that haven't happened yet."

"But I told you how much coffee costs." It's a weak argument, but I'm not sure I follow his logic.

"You did, but it will have no imminent effect on me. I won't be alive in the year 2023."

I feel every inch of those words as though each letter weighs a ton. Cole appears to be in his late twenties, and for him, it's 1934. He's right. He won't live to see 2023. He'll be lucky if he lives to see the 2000s at all.

It creates such a division between us. In here, Cole is alive —but when I step out that front door, he isn't.

Worry settles into the creases at the corner of his eyes. "Did what I say make sense?" he asks.

All I can do is nod. I don't trust myself to speak at the moment.

"Hmm," he hums, looking unconvinced. "I feel like I'm doing this all wrong. You still seem upset."

"I'm not upset."

"Sure you aren't, you liar." Cole winks. "Listen, I know you could tell me so many things. I could have a leg up on life if I let you fill me in on what's to come. But I don't want to live like that. The best parts of living are the parts that are a mystery. Look at you, for instance." He lifts a hand toward me.

"Me? How am I a mystery?"

"Oh, come on, Sylvie. How are you not? You showed up here out of the blue one day and later we learned we live in the same town one hundred years apart from each other." He chuckles. "Doesn't get more mysterious than that."

I wish he hadn't said the part about there being one hundred years between us. But he does have a point. "I think I get what you're saying. If you knew what to expect, there'd be nothing to look forward to."

He grins. "Now you get it. Everything would be all

mapped out and I would just be waiting for the next thing, knowing it was coming. I wouldn't want to live like that."

"That makes sense. I hadn't thought about it like that. I was thinking it would be more along the lines of having your fortune, with the added benefit of knowing everything I said was true." I smirk.

He runs a hand along the smooth counter. "It's tempting, but let's make a deal. Don't tell me anything unless I ask."

"I can do that."

"Deal?" He holds out his hand.

I look at it for a moment before taking it in mine. "Deal," I say. Cole moves our joined hands up and down while holding my eyes captive.

We're still holding hands when his mom comes bustling in from the kitchen. "Oh, sorry. I'm always interrupting, aren't I?" She looks away, embarrassed.

"You're not interrupting, Ma," Cole says. I would've expected him to drop my hand the moment his mom walked in, but he still has it in his grip. "Sylvie and I were just making a deal."

My eyes widen. I didn't expect him to say that, and now I'm wondering if he's going to tell her more.

His mom just smiles. "That's nice, dear." She turns her head to look at me. "Sylvie, so glad to see you again."

"I'm happy to be seen," I say, still holding Cole's hand.

"Everything okay?" Cole asks his mom.

She nods. "Oh, everything is just peachy." It's funny; where I come from, that expression is usually said with sarcasm, but Cole's mom seems to actually mean it. "Matter of fact, Mr. Yoder just delivered a box. I've got some peach crumb pies in the oven right now, but I need to get back home to your father. That's why I came out here. Would you mind keeping an eye on them? Shouldn't be much more than fifteen minutes. I wouldn't want them to burn."

"Sure thing, Mom." A look of understanding passes between them. There's something they aren't saying.

"Thank you, dear. And Sylvie, I'll see you again soon." She smiles sweetly, and then she's gone.

Cole lets go of my hand, and for a moment, I leave it out in front of me like it's frozen in place.

"So," he says, shifting his attention back to me. "Where were we?"

"Why didn't your mom ask any questions when you told her we were making a deal?" The words tumble from my mouth, and I wish I could grab them and shove them back in. I didn't mean to be so blunt. I should've danced around the question instead of just blurting it out.

But if Cole finds it intrusive, you'd never know. He smiles and looks back at the door where his mom just was. When his eyes are back on me, he answers, "I'm not really sure, to be honest. But if I had to venture a guess, I'd say she was just giving me privacy."

"Privacy?"

"Well, yeah. I mean, it's not every day she finds me holding hands with a pretty girl. I'm sure she was secretly thrilled." He winks, and I wish he wouldn't have. I feel it in places I shouldn't. And now I'm dying to change the subject.

"Did I hear talk of peach pie?" I lift a questioning brow.

He chuckles. "Caught that, did you?"

"Of course, I did."

"Well, come on," he says, tugging on the sleeve of my sweater. "Let's go make sure those pies don't burn."

CHAPTER TEN

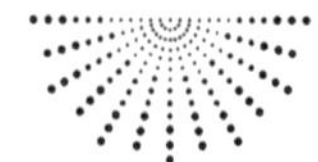

I have a set of salt and pepper shakers I bought at Williams Sonoma three years ago. There's nothing all that special about them. They're aqua and stand about four inches tall with rounded tops. The salt has more holes than the pepper. Nothing about them should hold my attention for longer than it takes to season my food, but I've been sitting here staring at the pepper shaker for the last ten minutes.

Or more like staring into it. I blink a few times, trying to shake off the disassociated stupor I've been stuck in. But it doesn't work.

All the blinking in the world can't explain why and how I can time travel. Lately, I've been stuck on the why.

I'm not so sure I'll ever understand the how, but the why? It feels like there must be a reason. Maybe there's a connection I'm just not making.

I don't know Cole's last name. I've never asked him, but it wouldn't be too hard to figure out. I found that article online about the cafe closing, but I couldn't bring myself to read it. I'm sure it lists his full name.

I drum my fingers over my lips, contemplating my next move. Do I search again? Maybe read the article this time? But suppose I do. Then I'll know something about Cole's future. Something that directly affects him. I'm not sure I'd be able to keep that a secret. More importantly, I don't think I want to know.

It's weird to think that right now, at this moment, Cole is no longer alive. It makes me feel physically ill. I tell myself that's because I've grown fond of him over the short time we've known each other.

But I think there might be more to it than that.

This crazy random happenstance where I somehow travel back in time connects us. We are tethered together, and all because I needed to dry off my pants one morning.

It's so random. If I had walked my usual way to work or stopped further back from the curb and out of the splash zone, we might never have met.

And now that we have, I wonder, have I interfered with the space-time continuum? Is Cole's fate somehow altered now? Is mine? The idea that I could've made such a catastrophic change in both our lives is not something I considered. But it's not like I had much choice that day.

Maybe this was always supposed to happen. I just wish I knew the reason.

I stand up from my tiny table and gather my plate and utensils. Scraping my uneaten eggs into the trash can, I decide I need a distraction.

Without thinking, I reach for the phone and call my mom. It rings four times before she answers. I picture her holding her phone and staring at my name as the call comes through, weighing her options. Today she decides to answer. Tomorrow, she might not. I've grown used to the wishy-washy attention I get from her. But it still doesn't stop me from hoping for more. The trick is to not get too over-anxious about it lest I end up getting hurt. I've been down that road too many times.

"Hi, Mom," I say as sweetly as I can.

"Oh, hello." Her voice is a step above a monotone. If I didn't know any better, I'd think that's just how she sounds. But I do know better. I've heard her talk to the cashier at a grocery store with more animation than this.

"How are you?"

"Okay," she answers and then pauses to yawn. She will yawn at least fifteen more times while we're on the phone. Again, if I didn't know any better, I'd think she was chronically tired. But really, she's just tired of me. I exhaust her. My existence is physically taxing on her. "How about you?" The question sounds more like an afterthought prompted only by manners. She doesn't really want a true answer from me.

Which is why I respond with, "I'm okay, too."

She hums into the phone, probably trying to sound glad. I'm sure she's aware of how a mother should behave with her child, and she's more aware of how far she falls from the norm.

I'm thinking about what to say next when she beats me to it. "How are things at work?"

She'll do this—ask me something about my life as a way of making me feel like she cares. This question carries with it a "see, I know your job is important" kind of attitude. And my job *is* important, but it's also all I have. She knows that, too.

"It's good. We've been busy."

"Busy is good," she says with a faint lilt. She's happy for the little extra morsel I fed her. It gives her the chance to sound interested.

"How's Dad?" I have to ask her since my father picks up his phone even less than she does. I haven't spoken to him in months. The last time he answered was clearly by accident.

He was trying to decline the call and accidentally accepted it. I could tell by the shock in his voice when he heard me on the line.

"He's well. We both are."

"Still taking your morning walks?" About a year ago, my dad had a health scare. He had a mini-stroke, and thankfully, he recovered quickly at home. Ever since then, he and my mom started taking walks in the mornings. It's made me happy just picturing them strolling around their neighborhood together. I know they got married because of me, but I think they genuinely like each other.

I've looked for things over the years to bring me comfort. With distant parents, you have to find your own version of contentment. My parents happy together is mine.

"Yes, we are." She's excited that I've asked her this. I can tell by the shift in her tone. She tells me about a new path near their house that leads to the park. "It's great because you don't have to cross any roads, and the only traffic you need to worry about is other people and bicycles."

"That's great, Mom. I'll have to check it out next time I visit."

If you've ever wondered if you can hear a frown, the answer is yes. I hear one when my mom responds. "Oh, um, were you planning to visit?"

"Not any time soon," I rush out, hoping to soothe her worry. It's crazy to think that other young adults have parents begging for them to visit while mine are fretting over it.

"That's good. Um, I mean, it's just that, well, your dad and I were thinking about renovating the bathroom, and I wouldn't want you to visit while we were doing that. What a mess that'll be." She chuckles, and it's fast and nervous.

"Didn't you guys just redo the dining room?" I know they

did, or at least that's what they told me they were doing the last time I mentioned I might visit.

"Uh-huh, yeah. Well, we just touched up some paint that had chipped."

So chipped paint equates to not allowing your daughter to come home for a visit. This is why when I tell people my parents don't like me very much, I say it with conviction. It's not something I question. It's something I know.

"Well, I should be going," she says without actually giving me a reason. There's a pause followed by another yawn. "It was nice hearing from you, Sylvie. Let's do it again sometime. Bye bye."

"Okay, Mom. Goodby—" That's all I'm able to get out before I hear the *click* of the line. I doubt she even heard me.

I set my phone on the table with a reverence it doesn't deserve. Aside from my communications with Mel, it's only ever brought me pain.

I've never planned on having kids. Not just because I don't have a partner. I've worried this dismissive gene might be hereditary. I'd like to think I wouldn't treat a child of my own this way, but I can't be sure. It could be ingrained in my DNA. I would never want a child of mine to feel the way my parents make me feel. Like I'm nothing more than a pebble in their shoe.

CHAPTER ELEVEN

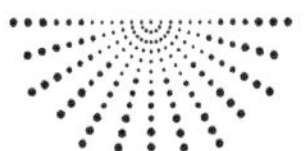

I haven't been back to the cafe in a few days. I'd like to say I've been busy, but the truth is, I've been wallowing. Phone calls with my mom are all the same. This last one shouldn't be any different as far as how it makes me feel, but watching Cole interact with his mom has me feeling sorry for myself. I'm grieving the loss of a relationship I never really had.

Mel knows this side of me. All I have to do is tell her I talked to my mom and she gives me a wide berth. She knows I'm in my head, and she also knows I'll come back eventually once I've processed my feelings. Or buried them.

But today is my birthday, and I don't want to be alone. So, I tug on the heavy wooden door and welcome the tinny little bell.

Cole has his hands in the display case, rearranging pies. The smile that blooms on his face when he sees me may be the best birthday gift I've ever received. It's nice when someone is genuinely happy to see you, and I let myself bask in the moment.

"There you are. I was beginning to wonder if maybe I'd imagined you." He smirks.

My cheeks grow warm under his gaze. I cross the room and sit on my favorite stool. He walks over to stand in front of me. Reaching across the counter, I give his arm a light pinch.

"What was that for?" he asks, chuckling.

"Just proving that I'm real," I say with a shrug and a cocky smile.

He leans over, taking my arm in his hand and turning it over so my palm faces up. Then, pressing a finger on my pulse, he holds it there for a few moments. I can hardly breathe. When he finally removes his finger, he looks up at me through dark lashes. "Yep, definitely real."

I lay my arm on my lap like it's suddenly fragile. Briefly, I remember when Bobby Reinhold brushed against my bare arm with his when we passed each other in the fifth-grade hallway. I swore I'd never forget that feeling. The warmth that took over, not only that small part of me that Bobby touched but over my whole body. It was like being warmed from the inside out. But where Bobby created a spark, Cole created an inferno.

"So, tell me, future girl, how've you been? I'm guessing you must've been busy since you haven't been here in a little while." He crosses his arms. The veins in his forearms dance from the effort.

The question makes me feel shy and foolish. I don't like being a victim, but that's exactly how I've been treating myself. A life devoid of family is still a life. And I've worked damn hard to get where I am.

Sensing my discomfort, he's quick to withdraw the question. "I'm only teasing, Sylvie."

"No, no, it's fine," I rush, flapping my hands. "I've just been a little preoccupied with life, but I couldn't let today go by without starting off my morning with Cole's famous coffee." I waggle my eyebrows.

"Your wish is my command." He darts around, prepping my coffee. As I'm about to take my first sip, he says, "Anything special about today?"

"Hmm?" I mumble, trying not to slurp the hot liquid.

"You said you couldn't let today pass without having my coffee. I just wondered if there was a special occasion I'm not privy to."

Sometimes Cole speaks and I'd never know he was from the thirties. But other times, his choice of words makes it glaringly obvious. "You know, I don't think I've ever heard another human actually use the word 'privy' in a sentence," I tease.

He cocks his head. "Is that so?"

"Mm-hmm." I nod. "But to answer your question, today is actually my birthday." I tell him in the same way I might say it's cloudy outside. I know the tradition that birthdays carry for people. For me, there's always been a little less fanfare. Still, I like birthdays. I think it's important to honor ourselves. It looks different for everyone, but I usually enjoy treating myself to things I like. And right now, Cole's coffee—or really just Cole—is at the top of that list.

"Hang on. Did you just say it's your birthday?"

"I did," I say, smiling.

"Sylvie. I wish I had known. I would've made your coffee fancier or had some kind of spectacular pie waiting for you." He starts looking around behind the counter like he may find a surprise gift stashed somewhere. It's so cute how he's acting like my birthday is this momentous occasion.

"Stop. Your coffee is perfect the way it is. And I don't need a special piece of pie. I am perfectly content with things just as they are."

He rests his arms on the counter and leans forward. "Please tell me you have special plans for the day."

I lift a shoulder in a half-shrug. "Does lunch with my best friend count?"

He nods. "Sure, but there's got to be more than that. What else are you doing?"

"Um, maybe grab some takeout for dinner and watch a show on Netflix?" I don't know why I say it like a question. Maybe because he's acting like I need some grand plans, and I feel like I'm not meeting his expectations.

"Okay, I have no idea what Netflix is, but it sounds boring."

"It's not bo—"

"Ah-ah." He stops me, holding up his hand. "Listen, here's what you're going to do. After work, go home and get changed into something fancy and come back here. I'm going to make you a birthday dinner."

"That's really not necessary," is what I say, but really, I'm thinking, "Oh my God, is he serious?" It would be incredible if he were, but also … is it a good idea? I'm already in danger of catching feelings for him. If he made me a private birthday dinner, it would probably push me over the edge.

"It's definitely necessary, Sylvie. This is your day. I won't have you spending it alone. That is … unless you wanted to be alone?" He chews on the corner of his lip.

"No, I don't need to be alone." I practically shout the words. Awesome. I'm sure he can hear the desperation in my voice.

But then he smiles and it's radiant. "Perfect. Then it's settled. Meet me back here at six thirty."

"It's a, um, deal." Whew. That was close. I almost said "date." Talk about embarrassing.

I finish my coffee and hop off the stool. Cole and I don't say goodbye this time. Instead, we smile and wave like we're suddenly nervous around each other. It's weird but also kind of exciting in the way that first dates often are.

When I reach the door, I turn and find him staring at me. "See you soon, Sylvie," he murmurs.

～

"So, anyway, Carlos was at my brother's yesterday—did I tell you this already?" Mel asks, pointing her breadstick at me.

"Nope."

"Good. 'Cause you know I don't like repeating myself. Anyway, so I walk in and Carlos was like, 'Yo, bro, your sister is a lot finer than I remember.'"

"He didn't?" I say, my mouth rounding.

Mel nods with authority. "He did."

"Wait, is Carlos the one you've been drooling over? Or was that Christopher?"

"Ugh," Mel groans. "No. That was Chuck. He was like four guys ago. And Christopher? Jesus, I haven't thought about him in months. Try to keep up, Syl."

I shake my head, chuckling. "Well, maybe if they didn't all have names beginning with the letter *C* it might be a little easier."

"Huh," she says, looking off into the distance. "That never even occurred to me before. Whoa. Maybe I do have a type!"

We both laugh.

The rest of lunch is filled with more entertaining conversation courtesy of my best friend. It's exactly what I need.

We picked our favorite Italian restaurant because they keep the breadsticks coming and never kick us out for staying past our welcome.

A few hours later, when we can't possibly eat any more gluten, we waddle out to Mel's car. "We timed this just right,

Syl. We'll get back to the office and only have an hour till we get to leave."

"A little birthday gift from me to you," I say with a cheesy grin.

She giggles as she starts the car. "So, what's on your agenda for later?"

"Later?"

"Yeah. What are your hot birthday plans? You have plans, right?"

I have no idea what to tell her. I don't love the idea of lying, but I'm also not ready to talk about Cole. What would I even say? "Well, I met this guy, and he's amazing. He's beautiful and funny and he makes a mean cup of coffee. Oh, and he's from the year 1934, so technically he's dead."

I end up answering with some "ums" and "uhs."

Mel shakes her head. "You have no plans. You're gonna go back to your apartment alone and watch Netflix, aren't you?"

"You say that like it's pitiful or something," I say, feeling defensive.

"Sweetie, listen, there's nothing wrong with spending some time alone, but you spend all of your free time alone." She reaches across the console and pats my hand.

"Not all of my free time," I argue. "I just spent the last two hours with you, although I'm starting to regret it."

She squeezes my hand before returning hers to the steering wheel. "Whatever. You love my crazy guy stories."

"You got the crazy part right," I tease.

"I know. I can really pick 'em, can't I?" She laughs. "See, this is why I need you to get out there. I can't be the only one with stories like these."

Oh, I've got stories. Ones I hope to share with her. Eventually. For now, though, I'm keeping them for myself.

CHAPTER TWELVE

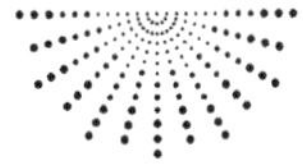

I tried on eight different outfits before settling on my trusty little black dress. It has thin straps, hugs me in a flattering way, and stops just below mid-thigh. But now, as I stand on the sidewalk, staring at the cafe door, I'm beginning to doubt my choice.

Cole told me to dress fancy, but I should've asked him to clarify. He's only ever seen me in my work clothes, which are usually simple dress slacks and a silky button-down.

I look down at myself and smooth my hands along the sides of my dress. What if it's too much or not enough?

I tug my phone out of my clutch and check the time. Shit. It's 6:28 p.m. Definitely not enough time to run home and change.

With a sigh, I grip the knob and give myself a mental pep talk. I look fine. It's just nerves.

When I open the door, I think I've made a mistake. It doesn't look at all like the cafe I'm used to. The lights are off, and the only illumination comes from candles. A few are dotted along the counter, and a larger one is in the center of one of the round tables.

I look around but don't see Cole anywhere. Taking tentative steps like the floor might cave in on me, I move toward the set table in the middle of the cafe.

The one familiar constant is the music. That low crooning trumpet is like a salve to my rapidly beating heart. It's calming in that comfortable kind of way, like a heated blanket on a cold night. A woman's voice sings soulful words that weave together with the melody. I smile, feeling warm and relaxed for the first time since leaving my apartment.

"There's the birthday girl." Cole's voice is the only thing more enchanting than the music.

I beam at him. "I can't believe you did all of this?"

"Don't give me too much credit. It's just a few candles." He lifts a shoulder.

"It's not 'just' anything. It's probably the nicest thing anyone's ever done for me. And it's perfect. So, don't sell yourself short."

"If you say so."

"I do," I say with a curt nod.

He chuckles. "Okay, then, why don't we get started? Here," he dashes out from behind the counter and pulls one of the chairs away from the table, "have a seat."

I do as I'm told, all the while trying to remember if anyone has ever pulled a chair out for me. I can't think of one person. Already this birthday is shaping up to be memorable, and we haven't even eaten yet.

"Sit tight and enjoy some bread," he says, gesturing to the basket on the table. "I'm going to go grab our first course."

He whisks away, disappearing into the kitchen. I lift the cloth from the basket and spy a small army of dinner rolls. Selecting one, I cover the rest back up and slather my bread with butter.

Cole comes back out a moment later carrying two salad

plates. "I figure we can start with bread and salad and then I'll bring out the main course."

"Sounds perfect."

"What do you think of the bread?" he asks.

"It's incredible."

He smiles. "It's my mom's recipe. I still can't believe I convinced her to share it with me. She won't even tell her sister! Actually, I have you to thank for it."

"Me?"

"Uh-huh. When I told her I wanted the recipe so I could make it for your birthday, she offered it right up."

My eyes widen. "Wow, I feel honored." I reach into the basket for another roll. "I have to ask though, why'd you make so many?"

"Oh, well, my mom told me to double the recipe. She said if dinner didn't turn out right, at least we could fill up on bread." He looks away sheepishly.

"Uh-oh, should I be worried?"

His chin juts back. "No, well, at least I don't think you should be …"

I giggle. "Relax, Cole. I'm just teasing you." I reach across the table and rest a hand on his arm. "I'm sure everything will be perfect."

He smiles widely.

I feel my finger slide a bit on the sleeve of his shirt. Cole must feel it, too, because he looks down.

"I had butter on my hand, didn't I?" I ask, feeling mortified.

He presses his lips together, stifling a laugh.

"And now there's butter on your shirt." I close my eyes and wish I could disappear.

Slowly, I lift my buttery fingers off his shirt and pull my arm away, but he rests his hand on top of mine, keeping it trapped.

I look up and find his eyes dancing with mischief. I scrunch my face, wondering what he's up to. A moment later, he lifts his hand from mine and dips his finger into the butter. I'm about to ask him what he's doing when he reaches up and dabs my nose. His finger glides off, leaving a small dollop of butter in its place.

I'm stunned speechless. I can't believe he just did that.

My eyes zing to his, and he sobers quickly. "Oh, shit. Sylvie, I'm so sorry. I was just trying to—"

I start laughing. It begins in small bursts but rapidly morphs into full belly guffaw type laughter. My eyes start tearing up, and my mascara is going to run, but I'm laughing too hard to care.

Cole looks shocked at first, but within seconds, he's laughing, too.

As we calm down, I grab my napkin and dab at my eyes. "I can't remember the last time I laughed so hard. Maybe never."

Cole's eyes sparkle. "It feels good, doesn't it?"

"Yeah, it does."

"You missed a spot."

"I did?" I ask, moving the napkin under my eye.

"Here," he says, picking up his napkin. "Allow me."

He dabs gently at my nose with the soft cloth, then he reaches over with his other hand, brushing his finger along my cheek. "There. That's better," he whispers. He doesn't pull his hand away. Instead, he allows it to slide down my face. He holds my chin with his thumb and index finger. "You look beautiful. I don't think I told you that, but I've definitely been thinking it."

My skin feels hot under his touch, and as much as I want to thank him for the compliment, I can't seem to find my voice. The moment is intense, and just when I think I can't take anymore, he withdraws his hand. I miss it immediately.

He stands so fast, I wonder if he's upset, but he mutters something about sauce, and dashes off.

I should've said something. He was vulnerable with me, and I just sat there like an idiot.

I'm pushing lettuce around on my plate when he comes back out. He's holding a plate with a silver domed lid. He sets it in front of me and pulls off the lid with a flourish. A perfect square of lasagna sits in the center. It's piled high with cheese and sauce and looks divine.

"You couldn't have known because I never told you, but lasagna is my favorite."

He grins. "I had a feeling."

"You did?" I narrow my eyes, and he chuckles.

"No, but it's my favorite, so I hoped you liked it, too."

I snicker. "Would you look at that. We may live in different centuries, but we still have things in common."

"Crazy, isn't it?"

"Super crazy," I agree.

We're openly flirting, and it's probably not the best idea, but right now, I don't care. It's just fun, and it's my birthday, so fuck it. Mel would be so proud.

When Cole sits down, we pick up our forks and take our first bites together like we're part of a synchronized dance.

"Oh my God, Cole. This is amazing." It's not polite to talk with your mouth full, but I can't wait for the chewing to be done. He needs to know how good this is. Besides, I covered my mouth, so it's fine.

"I'm so glad you like it."

I swallow the gargantuan bite I just took before speaking again. "Like it? No way. I love it."

He smiles so widely. Did he have dimples before? How did I not notice them? "Even better."

We continue eating, exchanging little anecdotes between bites.

"Wait, how old were you?"

"I was like three or four," I tell him.

"And it was just hanging out of your nose in front of everyone?"

"Uh-huh." I cover my eyes with my hand. "It's been twenty-four years and I still haven't gotten over it. That's real trauma for you."

"Well, it's understandable. You had a pussy willow dangling out of your nose. Did anyone even help you?"

"My teacher gave me a tissue, but the damage was already done."

"I should say so," he agrees.

"Your turn. What's your earliest most embarrassing memory?"

"Let me think on it," he says, tapping a finger against his bottom lip. He snaps his fingers. "Got it. Though I'm not sure I can bring myself to say this one out loud."

"Oh, come on! I just told you about snorting a pussy willow and sneezing it back out. Whatever story you have, it can't be much worse than that."

"It can be and it is," he says, grimacing. He scrubs a hand down his face. "Here goes nothing."

I rest my elbows on the table and prop my head in my hands. I don't think I've ever been this anxious to hear a story.

"The house we lived in when I was growing up had two bedrooms on the second floor. There was a bathroom in between them that you could access through a door in the hallway, but there was also a door in each bedroom that led to the bathroom."

"So, the bathroom had three doors?" He nods. "Interesting layout."

"It was a little odd, but as a kid, I liked not having to go out in the hallway if I needed to use the bathroom in the middle of the night."

I bob my head. "Well, sure. Dark hallways are terrifying."

"They really are," he agrees. "In this house, my brothers and I shared a room, and my parents were in the other room. On this one particular night, I woke up like I always did, needing to use the bathroom. I tiptoed inside so as not to wake up my brothers. Very little made my parents angry, but they had little tolerance for us being awake past our bedtime." He shivers like he remembers a time when he got in trouble for such a thing. I feel a pang of jealousy. I never really got in trouble when I was growing up. My friends thought I was lucky, but I never saw myself that way. I wanted what they had. Order and structure and parents who actually gave a shit. I was desperate for it.

"At first, this night was just like any other night," Cole continues. "I crept into the bathroom and closed the door carefully. But when I was in there, something stopped me from turning on the light. I realized my parents left their door open. I was just about to close it when I heard an odd sound coming from their room. It was a low moan like someone was in pain."

"Oh shit," I exclaim, clapping a hand over my mouth.

He nods solemnly. "Oh shit, indeed. But remember, I was five, so in my little head, I was sure there was an emergency. So, I ran back into my bedroom and shook my brother awake. He bolted upright and his eyes were so wide, I thought they might pop out of his head."

"What'd you tell him?" It's one of those questions I need answered, but I'm also afraid of the answer because I know it'll make me squirm.

He wrinkles his nose. "I said I thought something was wrong with Mom and that Dad was on top of her, shaking her up and down."

"No." I cover my eyes, peeking at him between my fingers.

"Yep."

"Then what happened?"

"My brother said we needed to go help them. So, the two of us went barging in there. We turned on the light and my mom screamed and then we screamed and my dad yelled, 'Boys! Get the hell out of here!' It was awful." He covers his face with his hands.

"I can't even imagine what you saw when you walked in there," I say, wincing.

"Everything," he says, letting his hands flop onto his lap. "We saw everything."

"Okay, you win. That was way worse than my story."

"You were warned," he says, steepling his fingers on the table in front of him.

He looks so sure of himself right now, and it's incredibly attractive, which is odd since I'm not normally lured in by an overly confident man. But the way he's looking at me—like I'm the next course—has me heating up in places I shouldn't be.

I close my eyes to put a bit of distance between myself and this situation. It only serves to heighten my other senses. My hands on my lap, fidgeting with the hem of my dress. My nose inhaling the heady aroma of burning candle wax. My ears picking up the soft melody of brass and soprano. I can feel my head swaying like I'm in a trance.

"Dance with me." My eyes spring open to find Cole standing before me, his hand outstretched and poised for me to take it. So, I do.

His fingers close over mine, gently tugging me up from my seat. He moves us to an open space between tables and turns to face me. Lifting our conjoined hands, he holds them between us while wrapping his free arm around my waist. My other hand rests along the nape of his neck.

At first, we only sway; the same way I was in my seat, slow and rhythmic. But as the music takes hold, our feet begin to move. I've only ever slow danced a few times in high school, and then it was sloppy and painful. I still remember the pain that shot through my foot when Jason Nolan stomped on it with his size ten Nikes.

This dance is different, much like everything else I've experienced when I'm with Cole. In a lot of ways, he feels like my first. The first guy I've ever been attracted to. The first to make me dinner. The first to hold my hand. The first to ask me to dance. The first to make me feel like I'm the only person in the room.

He pulls me closer so his mouth aligns with my ear. "Having a happy birthday?" he whispers.

"The happiest," I whisper back.

I close my eyes again, but this time, it isn't to escape. It's to savor. I never want to forget this moment.

The song ends, and the music tempo changes to a peppier beat. We slowly pull away from each other like it's the last thing we want to do.

"I have one last surprise for you," he says. "I'll be right back."

"I'll be here," I murmur. There's nowhere else I'd rather be.

CHAPTER THIRTEEN

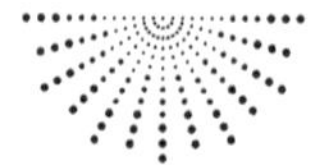

"Close your eyes," Cole calls from behind the kitchen door.

I do as I'm told, though I'll admit, I'd really like to peek.

"Are they closed?"

"Yep," I say as I clasp my hands together, feeling the weight of anticipation.

I hear the light tapping of his shoes as they move across the floor, and when I catch a faint whiff of cedar, I know he's close.

"Are you ready?" he asks, his voice just above a whisper.

"Mm-hmm."

"You can open your eyes now."

Sitting in front of me is a perfect pie with Happy Birthday Sylvie spelled out in icing. Lit candles line the perimeter.

I smile up at him, and his mouth falls slightly ajar. He reaches out, catching a strand of hair between his fingers. "The way your eyes catch the light from the candles makes it look like they're glowing," he says. His voice is heady as he tucks the strand of hair behind my ear.

My arms prick with goose bumps. I'm caught up in his adoring gaze, unable to pull myself away.

"Go ahead," he says. "Make a wish."

I blink and shake my head slightly, remembering that there's a lit pie in front of me. I look down at the tiny flames, wondering what more I could wish for, and then it hits me. There's one thing that would make this night perfect. Something I doubt any wish could make true, but I still close my eyes and focus on it as I take a deep breath. As I'm about to blow out the candles, the faint sound of singing catches my attention. Cole is kneeling beside me, quietly singing "Happy Birthday." His voice is deep and rich. It makes me wish even harder for something I can't have. I release the breath I've been holding and watch as the short flames flicker and extinguish, leaving trails of smoke in their wake.

"What'd you wish for?" he asks, craning his neck to look at me.

"If I tell you, it won't come true."

"Hmm." He looks back at the pie, watching as the smoke wafts from the wicks in thin streams until they disappear into the air. "I wonder if maybe we wished for the same thing."

"You made a wish, too?"

He smiles, keeping his eyes forward. "Sylvie, when I'm with you, I'm always wishing."

You know when you're in it, feeling your feelings and unable to think straight? Your emotions are so strong, they demand your attention. And you wonder if anyone else feels the way you do at that moment. I don't think I have to wonder. Cole has been leaving a trail of breadcrumbs for me with each word that comes out of his mouth. And I don't know what to do with them.

Cole tugs the candles from the pie. Bits of apple cling to

the bottoms. He sees me watching them. "Want a taste?" He holds a candle a few inches from my mouth.

I lean forward, wrapping my lips around the candle and sucking the filling from it. "Mmm."

Cole's eyes flare as they zero in on my mouth. I clear my throat, and he gives his head a slight shake.

He cuts into the pie and puts a large slice on a plate for me. "I'm afraid I can't take credit for this one. My mom made it special just for you. She wanted me to tell you she added a few extra shakes of cinnamon to make your birthday extra sweet."

"That's so nice of her. I'll need to thank her the next time she's here." The kindness Cole's mom has shown me makes me think of my mom. She didn't even bother to call and wish me a happy birthday. And this woman, whom I've only spoken to twice, made me a special pie. It makes me sad, but for the first time, I'm sad for her. She's missing out, and someday she may regret her choice to be so distant.

For a few minutes, the only sound besides soft music is the scraping of our forks against the plates. "I'd say your mom outdid herself, but I'm beginning to think she's just magical when it comes to baking."

Cole smiles. "It's true. No one quite makes a pie like her. She likes to joke that she's keeping me in business, but it's not much of a joke when it's the truth."

"Her pies are amazing, but so is your coffee. I'd say you two make a pretty good team and the success of your business is thanks to both of you."

"Aw, shucks. Sylvie, you're making me blush," he teases.

I lift a shoulder. "Joke all you want. It's the truth."

He smiles, and those dimples appear again. "Thank you. That means a lot coming from you."

I'm not sure why my opinion would matter, but it's nice to feel important. That's how Cole has made me feel this entire evening. Like I'm the most important person in the world.

The shadows from the candles dance along the walls of the cafe. I imagine the flickering shapes as people in the background, all here to celebrate my birthday. And here, front and center, with me is Cole. The person responsible for this magical evening.

"So, this is what birthday parties are like, huh?"

A deep crease forms between his eyebrows. "You say that like you've never had a party before."

"I haven't." I look away, feeling exposed. "But it's fine. That only helps me appreciate gestures like this one even more."

"Sylvie."

There's a reverence in the way he says my name. I expect to hear pity, but it's not there, and I'm grateful for it.

"Sylvie, please look at me."

As much as I'd like to meld my body into the wall right now, I can't ignore the pleading in his voice.

I turn my head, blinking slow and controlled. My eyes are filled with unshed tears, and I'm desperate to keep them from falling.

"You are extraordinary and you deserve to be celebrated. Not just on your birthday, but every day."

Shit. There goes a rogue tear cascading down my cheek. Traitor. I swipe at it, keeping my smile in place. "Thank you, but Cole, you hardly know me."

He shakes his head. "I know enough to want to know more."

My tears are no match for him. They begin falling more rapidly now and no amount of swiping gets rid of them.

Cole stands, grabbing his napkin. He walks around the table and kneels in front of me. He slides a hand under my jaw and carefully wipes my tears with his napkin. "You don't let yourself feel too deeply when it comes to your childhood."

I press my lips together and nod my head slightly.

"I know a thing or two about that as well."

I narrow my eyes.

"You've met my mom," he says, pausing to dab another tear. "She's exactly the kind of mom you'd expect her to be. And I can't honestly think of one thing I'd change about her. My father, on the other hand, well, he's different."

Cole sets the napkin on the table and stays kneeling in front of me. He takes my hands in his and turns them over, tracing the lines on my palms. "He was your typical father. Worked all day and came home for dinner. He doled out any necessary discipline and then sat on his favorite rocking chair with a pipe and his newspaper. I didn't know him all that much, but I knew what to expect from him. Until his accident."

Cole's throat bobs with a hard swallow. He continues his perusal of my hands, and I get the sense that he needs the distraction to help him tell the story.

"My dad worked for General Motors for years, mostly manufacturing parts for automobiles. His job consisted of assembly line work and there was some big machinery involved at times, too. One day he was working on a large machine and there was a jam."

I close my eyes, knowing what's coming.

"Yeah, you know where this story is going. I won't trouble you with the gruesome details. I'll just leave with this, don't stick your arm into a machine unless you've made sure it's been turned off."

I wince, and a shiver runs along my spine. "Oh my God. That poor man. What happened to his arm?"

Cole shakes his head. "Couldn't be saved."

"I'm so sorry. How old were you when it happened?"

"I was ten."

"That's young," I say, picturing the little boy who had to grow up fast. I can't even imagine what it must've been like for him to try to make sense of what happened to his dad.

"It was awful, that's for sure, but not nearly as awful as the years that followed. My father couldn't work after that, so he stayed at home while my mom waited on him." He works his jaw back and forth. "He'd bark orders at her and she'd do as she was told. And you know, that son of a bitch couldn't even be bothered to mutter a thank you."

He's no longer tracing the creases in my hands. He's still, almost statue-like. I lace our fingers together and give his hands a squeeze.

"The other day, when your mom said she had to get home to your dad, I noticed a look you two shared. It felt rude to ask at the time, but I had an inkling something happened to your father and that he wasn't well."

"Pfft, he's not well, all right. He's a bastard, is what he is. But my mom refuses to stand up for herself and she's begged me not to do it either. I guess that's the one thing she and I disagree on," he says through gritted teeth.

Even though I'm still getting to know Cole, I never would've guessed he had such a dark experience as a kid. It just goes to show, you only know as much about a person as they're willing to share.

"Thank you for telling me," I whisper.

He nods.

We stay like this—him on his knees, me lightly squeezing his hands—for a few more minutes. Both of us lost in our thoughts.

Cole slips his hands from mine and stands abruptly. "I'm sorry. I didn't mean to dampen the evening with my pitiful story."

I push out of my chair, standing toe to toe with him.

Looking up into his eyes, I say, "You didn't dampen anything, and your story isn't pitiful. It's real life and sometimes life just sucks."

He chuckles softly, shoving his hands in his pockets. "No truer words than those."

We stare into each other's eyes, keeping our hands to ourselves, though mine are itching to rake through his hair. This moment feels pivotal. The air around us crackles. The music still plays, providing a soundtrack rich with emotion.

His eyes are dark, so dark that if I were to go for a stroll inside them, I'd get lost on the first step. He rocks forward onto the balls of his feet as I rock forward on mine. We lean into each other, still keeping our hands from exploring. He tilts his head down as I angle mine up and back. He has at least five inches on me, but he must be stooping because our noses are practically touching now. If I were to lift onto my toes and he were to curve his neck a bit more, our mouths would be impossibly close. As if he can read my mind, his dark assessing eyes flick down to my mouth and then back up. My tongue darts out ever so slightly to moisten my lips. Did I imagine it or did his pupils dilate? His eyes are nearly black now.

A little closer and now our chests are touching. There's no pressure. We're barely making contact, but tell that to my heart. It's pounding so hard; I swear he must feel it through his shirt. I'm lifting onto my tiptoes without thinking it through. They're moving on their own as if my entire body is desperate for him. The closer I get to him, the more my heart thrums. My breathing increases, and my chest heaves. Anticipation like I've never known courses throughout my body.

Cole moves like a predator with his prey in sight. His movements are minuscule so as not to scare me off. I want to reach up and take his shirt in my fists, tugging him down to meet my waiting lips. But I keep my hands balled at my sides.

He lifts his hands and carefully places them on either side of my face. His fingertips slide into my hair. I raise my arms, my fists still tight, and place them against his chest. Cole's eyes flick between mine, and the right corner of his mouth curves. We move a little closer, and our noses touch. I can feel his breath on my face, warm and sugary sweet from the pie.

He tilts his head, and I tilt mine. Our lips are centimeters apart. When I was preparing for this evening, I never thought it would end like this. I was attracted to Cole, but I didn't think it would move past that. After all, we live in different centuries.

We live in different centuries.

I pull back and take a step away from him and then another. His eyes widen, and the curve of his mouth falls. One more step, and his hands no longer touch me.

"Sylvie?"

"I-I'm sorry. This is just … Thank you for the lovely dinner." I move sideways, walking around him, knowing if I get too close, I'll never leave. "I should go."

I reach the door and give one last glance back over the most wonderful birthday party and the most amazing man who gave it to me. And then I leave.

CHAPTER FOURTEEN

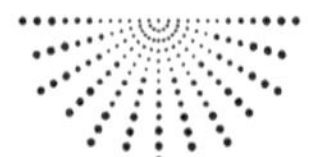

My breathing is ragged as I step out onto the sidewalk. For a brief moment, I look around, hoping my wish came true and I'm still in 1934. But then a cluster of teenagers walks past me, their eyes glued to their smartphones, and I know. There are no candles strong enough, no birthday wishes capable of giving me what my heart desires.

I trudge toward my apartment, keeping my gaze down. I'm afraid to look up. Afraid to make eye contact with anyone who passes me for fear that they'll see how dead I feel inside.

Inside my apartment, I feel the weight of being alone in a way I've never felt it before. It's nearly suffocating.

All this time, I've worked to earn my place in the world. I thought if I kept my grades up in school, I'd get into a good college and hopefully get a scholarship. When that worked, I upped the ante, signing up for extra lectures and graduating at the top of my class. I started working at Dylan and Forsyth Designs right out of college. I remember my first day like it was yesterday. I was given a tour of the building when I spotted the small office on the corner lined with windows. An older man by the name of Gerald was working at a walnut desk, and when he saw me, he smiled, introducing himself as the CFO. Allison corrected him on the spot. "Remember, Gerry, we don't use those repulsive titles around here. We're a team, and no one position is more important than any other."

He rolled his eyes when she wasn't looking and winked at me when he saw me notice. I let my gaze roam around his office and let my thoughts roam, too. The wheels were set in motion that day. I would sit in this office no matter how long it takes.

Turns out it took four and a half years. Gerry left for "greener pastures"—his words, not mine—and his office and his position were up for grabs.

Allison waltzed into the office I shared with two other people, asking to speak with me privately. "I think that office needs a woman's touch. What do you say, Sylvie? Are you up for the challenge?"

I've always been up for the challenge. That's how I've approached everything in life. But this challenge, where I've developed feelings for a guy who doesn't live in the same century as me, is one I'm not sure I'm capable of.

Mel would tell me to live it up. She'd say, "Emotions get in the way, Syl. Just have fun."

I've never been able to "just have fun." And it's too late for my emotions. They're what got me into this mess in the first place.

I flop down on my sofa with a groan. Why did Cole have to be so perfect? Why couldn't he have stayed two-dimensional and just been a guy who made great coffee? Instead, he had to go and have a great personality to match his great smile and his great eyes and his great fucking dimples.

And now I've blown it by running away. He put together

an amazing dinner for me, and I ruined it by bolting when we almost kissed.

I was just so afraid. Afraid of what would happen if we kissed. Afraid I'd like it too much. Afraid it would lead to other things … hoping it would.

"God, I am so screwed." I plunge my hands into my hair, scraping at my scalp with my nails.

My phone rings from inside my purse. I dig around and pluck it out. Mel's face is on the screen. She has impeccable timing.

"Hey, Mel." I'd love to sound happy or even just neutral, but my voice betrays me.

"Uh-oh. It's worse than I thought."

"What is?"

"You," she says, matter-of-factly. "I'll be right over."

She hangs up before I can object. And I'm glad. I could use a friend right about now.

Fifteen minutes later, the doorbell rings. I buzz Mel up and open the door to find her holding up a bottle of wine in one hand and two glasses in the other. "I'm here and I brought a friend."

"Come on in." I chuckle, feeling glad to see her.

With our wine poured, we situate ourselves on my couch. "All right, girly. Spill your guts."

I sigh. "I don't even know where to begin. Or how."

"Start with the part that bothers you the most and then work backward."

I almost laugh. The thing that bothers me the most is that I'm living in the wrong century. I don't think that's the best place for me to start. "There's this guy," I begin.

"I knew it!" Mel thrusts a fist in the air. "Good for you." A few seconds later, she changes her tune. "Or maybe not?"

"Eh, it's good, for the most part. I mean, he made me dinner for my birthday."

"Are you serious? That's so romantic, Sylvie."

I look away as my cheeks heat. She's right. It's the most romantic thing anyone's ever done for me.

"Okay, so what's the problem?"

"Well, we almost kissed, but then I got spooked and ran." I grimace, embarrassment settling on my chest like an anvil.

"You ran? Why?" Mel leans forward, watching me through narrowed eyes.

The story is so hard to explain, and any sane person will think I'm lying. "It's just that … we have no future."

"Sylvie," Mel says, trying to hold back a laugh. "You know you're not required to marry a guy just because you kiss him, right?"

"Yes, I know that." I roll my eyes.

"Good. So then, why are you so fixated on the future when you've got a guy who thinks enough of you to make you a special dinner for your birthday?"

"It's more complicated than that."

"So, uncomplicate it then."

She says that like it's the easiest thing in the world. If she only knew. There's nothing easy about this situation.

"Who is this guy, anyway? Have I met him?"

I shake my head. "No. Um, he owns that coffee shop. You know, the one I told you I recently discovered?"

"Oh, yeah, did you ever figure out what the deal was with Google maps?"

I sure have. And it's yet another thing I have no clue how to explain to her.

"Uh, yeah, it's a glitch or something. Anyway, Cole owns the cafe and we've become friends."

"Sounds like more to me," she says, lifting her brows.

I wave a hand. "Oh, I don't know. We get along well and he just wanted to do something nice for me. That's all."

"Uh-huh, sure. Listen, Syl, the guy made you dinner for your birthday. Was it just the two of you?"

I nod.

"And was there music and candles?"

Is she psychic or something? "Yes, there was. But it doesn't have to mean anything."

She tilts her head, studying me like I'm a lost cause. "Sylvie. I know you're not this clueless."

I sigh. "No, I'm not. But it doesn't matter anyway. I've ruined it."

"I'm sure that's not true."

"It's nice of you to say that, Mel, but you weren't there. I literally backed away from him and speed walked to the door like I couldn't get away fast enough."

"Okay, so you did a drastic thing. Undo it."

I scrunch my nose. "Undo it? How?"

"Apologize. Tell him you got caught up in the moment and started overthinking. If he knows you at all, that won't surprise him," she says snidely.

"Ha. Ha. Very funny." I pick up a pillow and toss it at her.

She bats it away, laughing. "You can fix this, Sylvie. I'm not even sure it's something that needs fixing. A simple explanation is all it'll take."

I bite at my lip. "You really think so?"

"Of course," she says with a tip of her head. "Now, tell me all about this guy. What's he like?"

I smile genuinely for the first time since leaving the cafe. Thoughts of Cole swirl in my head. "He's beautiful. He has this dark kind of unruly hair that's short, but not too short. It's enough that you could grab a handful if you tried. And his eyes are a deep brown, and depending on the moment, they're almost black. He has dimples, too. I only recently discovered those. And he's kind and a good listener. Gets along well with his mom. And he makes the best cup of coffee I've ever had."

"Why, Miss Sylvia Masters. I'd say you are quite smitten, girlfriend."

My mouth rounds. I don't know why what she's said shocks me. It shouldn't. I could speak about Cole for days and probably never run out of things to say. But smitten? Do I want to be smitten? It's a word that can only lead to trouble and heartache in this instance. But I think I'm too far along to stop it.

"Shit, Mel. I think I'm in trouble."

"That's kind of the way it goes. But I say, lean into it. You've found yourself a good one. Don't give up before things even get started. You deserve to be happy, Syl."

I smile at my friend. "Thanks, Mel. What would I do without you?"

"Oh, I think you'd be fine. It might just take you longer to figure things out, that's all." She grins at me.

"That's for damn sure."

"So, what's your plan? Are you going to go to him or are you going to stay away?"

I shrug. "I'm still not convinced being with him is a good idea, but I don't think I could stay away if I tried."

"There's your answer."

There's my answer. Be with Cole while I can, knowing full well it'll end eventually. But until it does, I "lean into it" as Mel so lovingly put it.

"Okay, I've taken up enough time. Catch me up on the Carlos scoop. What'd I miss?"

"Pssh, if you still think Carlos is in the picture, then you've missed a lot! But wait," she jumps up from the sofa, "this subject calls for more wine. Lots more."

CHAPTER FIFTEEN

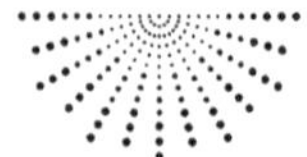

It feels like I'm always standing out here looking at the door to Cole's cafe, giving myself a pep talk. What do I even expect will happen if I go inside? I should leave.

I turn on my heel and start walking in the other direction, away from the cafe. I make it about five feet when Mel's words settle over me. I stop in my tracks, and an elderly man nearly collides into my back. He walks around me, shooting an angry look in my direction. I wince. "Sorry," I call out, but he doesn't acknowledge me.

I think about my life and how I've approached everything head-on. I didn't get where I am by running away.

And, at the very least, I owe Cole an apology. He celebrated me in a way no one ever has, and I took off running without so much as an explanation. He didn't deserve that.

I spin back around and march toward the cafe door, determined to make things right. When I tug the door open, I'm surprised to find the cafe buzzing with patrons. Three men sit at the table where Cole and I had our dinner. They argue over the correct way to lay concrete.

"Larry, you wouldn't know your ass from a hole in the wall."

"Oh yeah, well, I know how to pour concrete. Not that pig slop you try smearing all over the place."

Cole strolls up to the table, coffee pot in hand. "Fellas, fellas, listen, everyone does things a little differently. It's what makes the world interesting. Right, Frank?" He directs the last question to the one man at the table who's remained silent.

Frank gives him a quick nod, and Cole pats him on the back. "Atta boy. Now, here's some more coffee, and how about I get you guys each a slice of Ma's blueberry pie."

The men loudly agree, and Cole dashes off, never noticing me standing here.

A man and woman somewhere in their early twenties sit together at a round table against the wall. Their heads are bowed, nearly touching each other. The woman's mouth moves as she speaks, too quiet for me to hear. The man watches her like she's the only person in the room. It reminds me of how Cole looks at me. Well, how he looked at me.

There's another table with two older women. Both have their eyes on me. When I look their way, they both turn away. They whisper softly to each other, but I can't make out the words.

I feel out of place in a way I never have here before. I've only ever encountered a person here or there and Cole's mom when I stopped by. But right now, there are so many people, and I'm standing here feeling exposed.

The stools at the counter are empty, and I say a silent thank you as I tiptoe toward them. Sliding onto my favorite one, I clasp my hands together on the counter. Then I unclasp them and put them in my lap. Then I put one on the counter while leaving one on my lap. I'm a fidgety mess.

"That's fine, Ma. You can just leave the bin out. I'll put it away la—" Cole stops mid-sentence. His body is halfway in the kitchen and half in the cafe. His eyes are locked on me. They narrow slightly, and then he turns his head back toward the kitchen. "I'll take care of it later." He waltzes out of the kitchen, holding a pie in his hand.

I watch with rapt attention as he slices three pieces, placing them on small plates. He doesn't look at me while he's cutting the pie. Doesn't look up when he's taking the plates in his hands and balancing one on the underside of his forearm. Doesn't glance my way when he pushes out from behind the counter toward the table of rowdy men.

I look down at my lap. This was a mistake. Mel was wrong. He's not going to forgive me. And I shouldn't have come.

Slowly, I slide off the stool, straightening the strap of my purse on my shoulder.

"Leaving so soon? Don't tell me you're making another getaway."

I turn to find Cole standing behind me, an unreadable expression on his face.

"I, uh, you just seem busy. I didn't want to intrude."

"Intrude." He says the words slowly like he's tasting it. "Is that what you think you're doing when you come in here?"

"Well, no, but it's different today because—"

"Because I almost kissed you last night and you got scared and ran." He crosses his arms over his chest. His lips curve into something between a grin and a smirk.

I'm left stunned and unable to speak. He chuckles. "Relax, Sylvie. I'm just messin' with you. Go on. Have a seat." He juts his chin toward the stool, and I slide back down like an obedient child.

He walks back around so that he's behind the counter. I watch as he retrieves a cup and saucer from the counter.

Placing it in front of me, he fills it with coffee. "Have some of my coffee. I know you love it." He winks at me. I feel off balance. He's acting so strange. One second, I think he's upset with me, and the next, he's nearly flirting.

I do as he says and sip my coffee. He's right. I do love it, and it's a little like liquid courage because the next time I speak, there's no waver in my voice. "I'm sorry for leaving so abruptly last night. It really was an amazing evening."

"Until I—"

"Yes, you tried to kiss me as you so graciously keep reminding me." The corner of his lip twitches. He's enjoying this.

"So, tell me, Sylvie," he says, resting his forearms on the counter and leaning in. "Why'd you run?"

His close proximity is making me feel a little dizzy. I sit up slightly, putting a few extra inches of space between us. "Isn't it obvious?"

"Not to me."

I run a hand through my hair. He's going to make me spell it out. "We live in different centuries, Cole." My voice is barely above a whisper. I can't see the older ladies behind me, but I can feel their eyes on my back. They don't need to hear this conversation.

"Yes, we've established that. But what's that got to do with me kissing you?"

I shake my head. "It's not the kiss that I'm worried about. Well, not completely. It's what it could lead to."

"Sylvie, you're being a little presumptuous, aren't you?" He grins mischievously.

I close my eyes, sucking in a breath. Frustrated doesn't even begin to describe how I'm feeling.

He rests his hand on mine. I blink my eyes open to find his fixed on me. "I'm sorry," he murmurs. "I'm not trying to make you feel bad." He looks away for a moment. "Okay, maybe I am. Just a little." He chances a glance my way.

"I don't blame you. I never should've just left like that." My ears burn, and I'm sure if I could see them, they'd be bright red.

"No, that's not it. I get why you left."

I frown. "Wait. If you're not upset that I ran, why are you upset?"

"Because, Sylvie, when you leave, I can't go after you. I'm trapped here with no way to reach you. I watched you go last night without knowing if you'd ever come back. You can't imagine how helpless I feel."

I lift a hand, cradling the side of his face. "I never thought of that. God, Cole, I'm really so sorry."

His eyes dance with mine. "It's okay."

"No, it's not. If that were me, I'd be going out of my mind."

He chuckles. "I was."

I look down at the counter, unable to meet his eyes. "Hey," he whispers. "It's okay. Really. You came back. That's all that matters."

I stare deep into his eyes. "I promise I'll always come back. As long as it's possible, I'll never be gone for good. And if, for some reason, I can't come back, I'll make sure I say goodbye, okay?"

He smiles and opens his mouth to reply, but he doesn't get the chance.

"Who's this? Cole, you been keeping this girl a secret?" One of the concrete guys appears beside me. I release Cole's face and drop my hand in my lap.

"Mitch, this is Sylvie. Sylvie, this is Mitch." Cole's introduction is short, and I can tell he's hoping it'll satisfy Mitch.

It doesn't.

"You know, come to think of it, I don't think I've ever

seen you with a girl. Are you two, uh, serious?" Mitch's eyes drop to my chest. My button-down doesn't reveal anything, but I still place a hand against my sternum.

Cole clears his throat, but Mitch takes his time peeling his eyes away from me. "Sylvie is a friend. Are you and the guys getting ready to head out?"

Mitch turns to look back at the table where his friends are sitting. "Yeah, we got a job up north. Probably won't be back this week."

"Hope it goes well. Good seeing you guys." There's a dismissive tone in Cole's voice, but Mitch doesn't seem to pick up on it.

He taps his hand on the counter and starts heading back to his table to collect his jacket. Before he makes it there, he stops, looking back at me. "I gotta say, it was very nice meeting you, little lady. Hope to see you again."

I don't respond.

When I look back at Cole, he's practically sneering. "Ignore him," he says through clenched teeth.

"I am, but Cole, maybe you should take your own advice," I say with a shit-eating grin.

He looks at me with wide eyes. "Well, well, well, look who's got her fire back."

I chuckle. "What can I say? I was worried you'd hate me, but now that I know you don't, I'm feeling pretty good."

"Sylvie, I could never hate you."

"Never say never," I mutter, looking down at the counter.

He touches my chin, lifting my face with the pad of his finger. When we're eye to eye, he whispers, "Never."

The soulful music I've come to love wafts from the speaker in the corner, and the hushed murmurs of customers flow around us. All of it is background noise. Nothing is louder than the beating of my heart, and nothing is clearer than Cole's intentions. He wants what he wants, centuries be damned. And I'm slowly starting to agree with him.

A dainty throat clears behind us, but it's enough to snap us out of our trance. We both blink ourselves back to reality. But we don't separate. We stay close together, turning our heads at the intrusion.

One of the older ladies is standing there, watching us closely. Her smile is barely contained, though she blots at her lips with a handkerchief in an attempt to mask it. "Pardon me, but Cole, sweetie. Eras and I wanted to settle up with you. We need to leave in a minute if we want to make it to Bridge on time."

"Sure thing, Mrs. Wilder. Give me just a moment, and I'll ring you up." Cole rushes over to his gargantuan cash register and begins pressing buttons. Mrs. Wilder stays where she is, not even attempting to mask her stare.

I flash a shy smile and lift my hand in a small wave.

The smile she returns is wide, so wide I can see a gap between two of her teeth in the back left bottom row. "Hello, dear. It's mighty fine to meet you."

"Hi, Mrs. Wilder. I'm Sylvie."

"Sylvie. That's a pretty name for a pretty girl. I've been watching you and I'm just so glad Cole has himself a lady. You two sure look sharp together."

She thinks we're a couple. "Oh, we're not—"

"Okay, Mrs. Wilder. That'll be seventy-five cents."

Mrs. Wilder fishes the money out of a tiny change purse shaped like a butterfly. She pays Cole, and when she turns to leave, she winks at me. There's no point in trying to explain the situation to her.

I can't even explain it to myself.

"Listen, Sylvie," Cole says, pulling my attention back to him. He stands with his palms flat on the counter, forearms flexing, jaw hard. From my vantage point, he looks like a force to be reckoned with, but when he speaks, his voice is anything but confident. "How do you feel about coming back here when I close up? I was thinking I could show you around town a little. It's not every day you get the chance to explore your city a hundred years in the past." The smile on his face is crooked as he waits for my answer.

I don't know what to tell him. On the one hand, I'd love to spend more time with him, and getting a chance to see the town in 1934 would be pretty amazing. But on the other hand, it feels like I'm setting myself up to fall flat on my face.

"I can tell by your face that you're conflicted. So, here's what I want you to do. Take all of those doubts and shove them aside. Now just say the first word that comes to mind."

"Yes," I say without hesitation.

His smile is brilliant, and even though I can't see myself, I know mine is, too.

That should be my first sign that this is a colossal mistake. But right now, I don't give a shit.

CHAPTER SIXTEEN

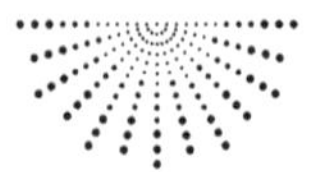

"Good morning, Mel," I say, tapping her desk as I stroll past.

"Morning!" she calls. I can hear the pounding of her feet as she follows me into my office.

She plops into the chair opposite my desk. I take my time, putting my purse away in my desk drawer and taking my jacket off. I'm draping it on the back of my chair when she explodes, "Oh my God! Will you please just sit down and tell me what happened this morning? I've been waiting on pins and needles for the last hour!"

I sit down and glide my chair toward my desk. "I went to see Cole this morning."

"Yeah, yeah, I figured out that part when you were late getting here. Tell me what you said and then tell me what he said and then tell me what you said when he said what he said!"

A laugh bubbles out of me. "You are really invested in this, aren't you?"

"Are you serious right now? You finally have a story to tell and it turns out, you suck at storytelling."

I shake my head. "Would you relax? Everything went really well this morning. Actually, better than I hoped. Happy?" I raise my eyebrows.

"Marginally," she says, rolling her eyes. "It's a start, but I'm gonna need more detail than that."

I fill her in, starting from the beginning while leaving out the parts about time travel. I'm not sure she's ready to hear about that. Mostly, I'm not sure I'm ready to say it out loud.

I tell Mel that Cole wants me to come back when he's closing up today.

"What time is that?"

"Two o'clock." My eyes flick to the clock on the wall. "Which is less than five hours from now."

"What'd you tell him? You better have said yes."

I smile. "I did, though I'm still not sure it was the right decision."

"Pssh, of course, it is. And it's perfect because you have that meeting with Allison this morning and then the rest of your day should be smooth sailing. Perfect for bowing out early."

"Who's leaving early?" Jackie snivels from the doorway.

"Should've closed the door behind me," Mel mumbles under her breath.

"Good morning, Jackie," I say in my best business casual voice. "What brings you by?"

"I thought I might sit in on your meeting with Allison this morning. After all, two heads are better than one," she chirps.

"Hold on, how did you know Sylvie has a meeting?" Mel glares at Jackie.

She just lifts a shoulder. "What can I say? Word around here travels fast. But not half as fast as you, Sylvie. I couldn't help but overhear—"

"Yes, you could," Mel quips.

Jackie shoots daggers at her, and then quickly masks her

face with a smile. "You're leaving early, again? Wow. Well, good for you. Don't want to work yourself to death. I should know, I'm always here. I mean, just the other day, Allison said, 'Jackie, you are so dependable. You're always here.'"

"Allison didn't say that. I call bullshit." I've gotta hand it to Mel; she just says it like it is.

Jackie ignores her, keeping her eyes trained on me. "Anyway, as I was saying, I can join you this morning. My schedule is free."

"Thank you for the offer, Jackie, but that won't be necessary." She watches me, waiting for an explanation, but I don't offer her one. The meeting is between Allison and me. She has no business sitting in, and she knows that. I can spot what she's planning a mile away.

She plasters a fake pout on her face, and I want to gag. "Suit yourself. But if you change your mind, you know where to find me."

Mel stands. "We all do, unfortunately. Now, run along, Jackie. Sylvie has loads of work to do." She keeps walking, forcing Jackie to back up, and once they've stepped into the hall, Mel reaches back to push my door shut, throwing me a wink right before she gives it a shove.

What would I do without her?

My meeting with Allison goes smoothly, despite a hiccup right at the beginning. Jackie placed herself in Allison's office before I arrived, and when Allison mentioned we had a meeting, Jackie offered to stay. Imagine my delight when Allison told her no, adding this was a matter that "Sylvie is more than capable of handling on her own."

I'm not usually one to gloat, but the look on my face must've been triumphant because the glare Jackie shot me on her way out was sharp enough to cut glass.

With my meeting out of the way, I typed up a quick report that Allison requested. She wanted some preliminary numbers for the new strip mall. Once that was finished, I emailed it to her and glanced up at the clock.

Crap. It's only 12:30 p.m., but you know, I didn't take lunch, and I rarely ever take time off. So, without giving it another moment of thought, I rise from my chair, collect my things, and waltz out of my office, stopping at Mel's desk.

"Leaving even earlier? You're gonna go home and get all spruced up, aren't you?" She starts clapping frantically. "Oh! I'm so excited for you!"

I giggle and almost cover my mouth, but then I decide, fuck it. I deserve to be happy and happy people giggle.

There's a bounce in my step as I head to the elevator. My mood is hard to describe, but if I had to, I'd say it's somewhere between delighted and shitting bricks. But probably a little more on the delighted side.

At home, I change into a dress that errs on the longer side. It's navy with cream lace edging. It's a bit vintage and a little cottage core. It feels perfect for the occasion. I'm aware that I'm living in an entirely different time as far as fashion goes, and the last thing I want to do is stand out too much when Cole is showing me around town.

Cole is showing me around town. My town, but in 1934. This is wild. What even is my life right now?

I head to the cafe, bouncing on the balls of my feet as I walk. I pass a few people on the way, and I smile at every single one. A few smile back and a few don't. One even glares at me, but I'm too excited to care.

When I reach the door, I grasp the knob, feeling the cool metal against my skin. Taking a moment, I inhale deeply and let it out. "You're just having fun, Sylvie. That's all." I could whisper those words to myself over and over, and I still wouldn't believe them.

Cole is wiping off a table when I walk in. This is the cafe I'm used to, no one here but us.

He looks up, taking me in. "Sylvie," he says, his voice barely above a whisper. "You look … stunning."

I glance down, trying to imagine myself as he sees me. I thought I looked fine when I left my apartment, but he's looking at me like I could stop traffic.

"Thanks, um, you look good, too." He always does. I never thought much about a man in an apron before, but I'll never make that mistake again. Trust me when I say it just does things to me.

He chuckles. "You saw me earlier. I haven't changed."

I walk toward him. "You looked good earlier, too."

He looks down at the table he's been wiping. Is he … yep, he's blushing, and he's trying to hide it from me.

"Sorry. I'm a little early."

"Don't be sorry. I mean, clearly, I'm busy, but it's fine." He waves a hand around the empty cafe.

I snicker. "The place was pretty full earlier. Did it stay that way the rest of the day?"

He shakes his head. "No, that was just the morning rush."

"I don't think I've ever seen it so full." I look around, remembering the different people who were there this morning.

"It was a typical morning crowd, but you're usually here before things pick up."

I nod. We're making small talk, and it's weird. I don't know why I feel so nervous all of a sudden. Conversation between us is usually pretty easy. However, something about our looming plans has me a little on edge.

"Do you need more time to clean up? I could help." I look around for another rag or a broom.

"No, it's fine. Don't worry about it. Actually, I think I'll lock up now and just finish my cleaning later."

"Are you sure?"

"Positive." He grins. "I'm anxious to show you what your town looked like a hundred years ago."

"This is kind of crazy, right?"

"Kind of," he says with a nod. "But also, fascinating."

"Wildly fascinating," I agree.

He walks the rag over to the sink behind the counter, rinsing it off. When he's finished, he turns to me. "Ready?"

"As I'll ever be."

"Come on." He bends his arm, inviting me to thread mine through the crook of his elbow. I walk toward him and link my arm in his. "Shall we?"

"We shall."

With our arms joined, we push through the door into the kitchen and head to the exit.

"Here goes," Cole says, his hand poised to turn the knob.

"Nothing," I mutter.

"Huh?"

I shake my head. "I was just, um, it's a saying. 'Here goes nothing.'"

"I thought that's what you said. But it doesn't work here."

I scrunch my face.

He smiles. "Here goes everything." And with that, he turns the knob, and a burst of warm air hits me in the face. I breathe in, catching a whiff of gasoline and popcorn and maybe a hit of a campfire.

"The thirties smell good. Is there a movie theater nearby?"

"As a matter of fact, we have a picture palace around the corner."

"Picture palace?"

Cole chuckles. "I'll show you."

We stroll along the sidewalk arm in arm, catching a few glances, but none that linger. I chose my outfit well and don't look like too much of an outsider.

When we round the corner, I can hardly believe my eyes.

In front of us is a theater of grand proportions. A large billboard-style display has the words "It Happened One Night Starring Clark Gable" in dark block letters. Gold fixtures adorn the front of the building and a bevy of lights surrounds the sign. It's gaudy but also incredibly beautiful.

"Wow," I whisper. "Theaters in my time are not nearly this impressive."

"No?"

"Uh-uh. They're just plain white brick buildings. Some have lights and a sign, but nothing this dramatic. Now I see why you call them palaces."

He chuckles. We stand there for a few minutes, looking up and down the street. "Recognize where you are?"

I squint, surveying the buildings. After a minute or so, I shake my head. "It feels vaguely familiar, but the differences are too much for me to place where I am."

"Windsor and Maple," he says.

"Hmm?"

"That's where you are. At the corner of Windsor and Maple."

I slide my arm out from his and turn in a circle. "Oh, yeah," I say, my voice full of wonder. "Now I see it. Though, none of this is here anymore, aside from that building over there." I point to a large red brick building on the corner. "Except it's not called Mervyn's. It's a Whole Foods now."

"Is it weird seeing things this way?"

"Absolutely," I say without hesitation.

He nods, a sober look on his face. "I imagine it must be."

We're silent for a moment, and I wonder what he's thinking. I know what I'm thinking. We need a distraction, something to take some of the strangeness out of the situation.

"What do you say we go inside?"

"Where?" he asks, cocking his head.

"In there," I jut my chin across the street. "The picture palace."

He smiles so widely, his dimples are prominently displayed. If I'm not careful, those dimples could be my downfall. "I'd say that's a grand idea. Let's go." He offers me his bent arm and I take it. We race across the road and stop in front of the ticket counter.

I can't stop smiling. This feels like a dream.

CHAPTER SEVENTEEN

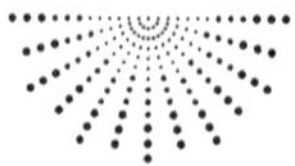

"This place is massive," I whisper to Cole.

"It's a palace, remember?" he says, winking.

He's not kidding. It really is. Everything is gold and shiny. Even the ceiling is decorated with gold trim. The carpet is loud and full of colorful swirls. The walls are covered in thick paper. It's a deep red with a black damask pattern. I'm not an interior decorator, but something tells me Allison would have a conniption with all these clashing patterns. Still, in here, it works for some reason.

Rows and rows of seats fan out from a glowing white screen in the front. The seats are stadium style, with each row on its own step.

Cole leads me down the aisle, stopping about ten rows from the front. We slide into an empty section and position ourselves so we're centered with the screen.

Once we're seated, I can't stop looking around. My head swivels left and right as I take in the room. "This is extravagant."

"It adds to the thrill of seeing a motion picture. When

you're sitting in a place like this, you know you're about to witness something special."

His face is animated as he talks, and it's not hard to see he loves movies. I've always enjoyed them, but watching Cole talk about it like it's some incredible experience has me thinking, have I ever felt that way about anything? No. I don't think I have. I don't have hobbies or even small things I enjoy outside of work.

"You know," Cole says, leaning over to whisper in my ear, "you wear every emotion on your face."

I suck in a breath, turning to him with wide eyes. "I do?"

"Mm-hmm. And right now, you look utterly miserable. Would you rather not see a movie?"

"No, no, it's not that. I was just sitting here listening to you talk, and it's obvious you get a lot of joy from going to the movies."

"I do," he says, carefully enunciating the words as though the admission is something he should be ashamed of.

"I think it's wonderful that you have something that brings you joy outside of your everyday life."

"What brings you joy, Sylvie?" He nudges my shoulder with his.

I glance down at my hands in my lap. "That's just it. I don't know. And I guess I was just feeling a little sorry for myself after that revelation."

He reaches over, taking my hand in his. "Maybe you just haven't been looking hard enough."

Or maybe I've just been looking in the wrong century. I don't say it out loud, but I'm practically screaming it in my head. Joy is something I've been missing. I've been distracting myself with accomplishments, but really, when it boils down to it, those high honors don't keep me warm at night or give me something to look forward to.

But I look forward to seeing Cole and find joy in talking to him. And I don't know what to do with that.

Thankfully, I don't have to think about it now because the theater lights begin to dim, and the movie starts.

When the lights come on, everyone in the theater claps. It takes me a moment, but I join in. It's so different from what I'm used to, but it makes me wonder why we ever stopped clapping for movies. It makes sense, considering we've just been entertained.

"What'd you think?" Cole leans over, and his lips brush against the shell of my ear, sending goose bumps down my spine.

He held my hand for the whole movie. At first, it was hard to focus on anything besides that. But once the story picked up, I was riveted.

The entire film was in black and white, something I'm not accustomed to. It took a few minutes to get used to it, but pretty soon, I didn't even notice. The theme was enemies to lovers, a classic romance trope and one I'm a fan of. There was so much angst and tension; I was on the edge of my seat for half of it. Claudette Colbert and Clark Gable were electric together. But I think what I loved the most was knowing how it would end. There's only one way for movies like that to end—with a guaranteed happily ever after.

The theater is almost empty, but Cole and I remain in our seats. Turning to him, I ask, "Do you think there is such a thing as happily ever after?"

"No," he answers without hesitation.

"No?"

"No," he says again, sounding certain. "Don't get me wrong. I think it's possible to be happy for most of your life, but not for all of it. It's not realistic."

I nod, staring off into the distance, thinking about what he said. He has a point. Even though I'd like to believe in happily ever after, I know it's not real life. "But don't you think you could find someone who could make you happy every day?"

He chews at his bottom lip. "I don't know. Maybe?"

"Hmm."

"You don't agree?" He cocks his head.

"No, I agree. I just don't want to, is all."

He nods. "Understood. And hey, I'm always up for being proven wrong."

"I'll remember that," I tell him with a shrewd smile.

"I'm counting on it."

A throat clears nearby, and we turn to find an usher holding a broom with an expectant look on his face.

We mutter a few apologies and hustle out of our seats. As we dash down the aisle, we can't help but laugh. There's just something about getting in trouble as an adult that immediately makes you feel like an unruly teenager.

When we're outside, I look at Cole. His cheeks are flushed, and I'm sure mine are, too. "You're a bad influence," I say, giving him a playful poke in the arm.

"Me?" He presses a hand to his chest. "You're the one who wanted to have a philosophical discussion in an empty theater."

"What can I say?" I shrug. "The movie had an effect on me."

"You liked it then?" There's a hopeful lilt in his voice.

"I think that's a safe assumption," I say, grinning.

"Excuse me, please," a deep voice bellows from behind me. Cole grasps my shoulder and tugs me toward him. My body collides with his, and he wraps an arm around me. A large, brusk man sidles past us. I watch after him as he rushes down the sidewalk.

"Guess he was in a hurry." When I glance up at Cole, I find him impossibly close. My heart thuds in my chest.

"I guess so," Cole says softly. He stares down at me for a moment. Then, he lifts his hand and runs a finger along my forehead, pushing a stray hair off my face.

I'm not sure if he's leaning in or if I am. Maybe we both are. Our mouths are inches apart.

"Pardon me," a woman calls from Cole's right. She brushes past, bumping his arm with her elbow. It jostles us and is enough to snap us back to the present.

"I guess we should keep walking. I get the distinct feeling that we're in the way," he jokes.

I chuckle, but I can't ignore the disappointment I feel. Another kiss interrupted, and this time it wasn't me. I was ready to give in. Giving my head a slight shake, I take Cole's proffered arm. "Where to next, Mr. Tour Guide?"

"Hmm," he says, glancing around. "Would you like to see where I live?"

My insides react immediately, vibrating with excitement. My expression must not match because he starts to backpedal. "That is, uh, we don't have to if you don't want to."

"No, no, I do." I rush the words, earning a toothy grin from him.

"Okay, then. It's only a short walk this way." He juts his chin toward the sidewalk in front of us.

"Perfect. Lead the way."

We arrive at a brownstone with dark green shutters. There are three concrete steps leading up to the front door. A few potted plants and a small wooden bench sit atop the charming little porch. Cole seems nervous as he un-threads our arms and fumbles in his pocket for his keys.

I watch as he eventually selects the right key and fits it into the lock. He wears a sheepish grin as he turns the knob and pushes the door open. "Um, please forgive the mess. I meant to tidy up a bit, but I wasn't exactly sure I'd have company." He scratches the back of his head as he moves aside for me to pass through first.

I'm not sure what he considers a mess, but I see nothing out of place. In fact, it's spotless. The furniture is a little sparse, but it's cozy and warm. The living room is off to the right of the foyer, and it's especially inviting with its dark walls and stone fireplace. I stroll in and around the room, stopping every so often to look at some books on a shelf and a few paintings on the wall.

I look behind me to find Cole watching me closely. "This place is incredible."

"It was my grandmother's. I'm afraid I haven't done much updating, but truth be told, I haven't wanted to change much. Being in this house reminds me of when I was young and used to come and stay with her. It's comforting," he says, lifting a shoulder.

Who is this man, and why does he have to live in the past? He's an empath and a romantic, and I hate how much I want to kiss him right now. He's vulnerable and the lack of confidence is alluring.

I cross the room and wrap my arms around him. It takes him only seconds to reciprocate. We stand together, holding each other. I wanted to comfort him, but I didn't realize I needed comforting, too.

Cole's face rests on the side of my head. "Why do you think you can time travel?" he asks, his mouth moving against my hair.

I close my eyes, mulling over the question I've been asking myself every day. "I honestly don't know."

"We may never know," he says, pulling me closer. "But I don't think it matters."

"You don't?"

"It only matters that you're here. The how and the why

are inconsequential." He pulls back just enough to look at me.

I stare deep into his eyes, getting lost in the dark abyss. There are no distractions in here. Nothing to come between us. Nothing to stop this moment that we've been racing toward for days, maybe even weeks.

I lift up on my toes. Nothing about what happens after that is slow. His lips crash into mine. We collide like this kiss will somehow give us answers. We move together like we were always meant to do this. His mouth captures mine, and it makes me wonder about all the other kisses I've ever had in my life. Were we doing it wrong? Because I've never felt a kiss surge through every bit of my body before, but I can feel this one in my toes and in my fingers. My ears tingle, and my stomach swirls. I feel it in other places, too. Places demanding to be touched.

Cole threads his fingers into my hair, gripping it at the scalp, tugging just enough. A moan slips out of my mouth, and he turns feral. My hands slide up his chest, taking his shirt in my fists. We're holding on to each other so tight, like we're afraid the other might disappear.

I don't know what any of this means. I don't know why I'm here or how long I'll be able to cross into this time period. But right now, I don't care. I feel more alive now than I ever have. The joy I was missing is here.

CHAPTER EIGHTEEN

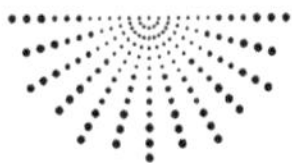

ole is shuffling around the cafe, picking up chairs and turning them upside down on tables. I've offered to help, but he says he's got it. I think he's only saying that, so I'll stay sitting on the counter. He keeps stealing glances at me, a hungry look in his eyes.

After the scorching, life-altering kiss we shared, I thought more might happen. But Cole is nothing if not a gentleman. He slowed the kiss down until, finally, we stopped. He placed a single kiss on the tip of my nose and then backed away from me.

He gave me a tour of his home, and we shared a plate of cookies and milk. It was sweet, but I kept wishing we could get back to where we were.

I've been afraid of this connection we have only because I worry about my heart. But the heartbreak is worth it if it means I get to live in this dream world a little longer, indulging in things that make me happy.

He heads to the kitchen and returns a moment later with a broom. He's sweeping up the day's dirt while a soft trumpet and crooning voice waft from the radio.

There are times when I'm here that I forget it's 1934, but not now. Cole is wearing brown pants with a cream-colored button-down shirt. He has his sleeves rolled up in that way that makes me starry-eyed. Dark brown suspenders are clipped into the waistband of his pants. He looks like a man from the past. It makes me wish I were a woman from the past, too.

He brushes the broom around the cafe floor, pushing the debris to the center. Once it's all gathered, he reaches for the dustpan and small brush on a nearby table.

I make a habit of cleaning my apartment weekly. I enjoy it when things are orderly, though not the act of cleaning itself. But something about Cole bent over, collecting the dirt from the day, has me completely mesmerized.

He empties the dustpan into the trash can behind the counter and then washes his hands. He comes back out to collect the broom.

"You keep this place so tidy; I bet you could eat off the floor."

He rests his hand on the top of the broom handle. "You could, but I'm not sure why you would want to."

I lift a shoulder. "You could be a trendsetter. Think about it. There are cafes in every town, but none that serve their food on the floor. Your cafe would be memorable."

He frowns. "You don't think it's memorable now?"

I scrunch my face. "No, I didn't mean—"

He stalks toward me, not stopping until his thighs bump against my bent knees. My hands press against the counter on either side of my bottom, bracing for what he has planned. And he does have something planned. The gleam in his eye gives him away.

"Perhaps I should do something to make it more memorable." A wicked grin curls on his face.

He moves a little closer, and my knees part to give him room. He takes it, inching even closer. He's taller than me, but with me sitting on the counter, we're at the same height. He cradles the side of my face in his hand. His eyes flick back and forth between mine. I lick my lips in anticipation of what's to come.

He leans in, resting his forehead on mine, rocking it lightly side to side. "I was happy running this place on my own, keeping it in the family. It felt like my life had a purpose. But then you came bursting through that door, sopping wet and needing to use my restroom. I didn't know what it meant at the time, but something happened deep inside my chest, and for the first time, I felt a flutter like my heart was skipping beats or maybe it was doubling them. Now I wonder how I ever could've thought I was happy before. I don't think I even knew what happy felt like until I met you." His voice is soft, but his words have more weight than words are meant to have.

I know exactly what he's feeling because I'm feeling it, too. Except I don't think I ever was happy. I was too busy chasing the next big thing to realize that happiness was never going to be something I could earn. Instead, it's something I discovered. "Why do we have to live in different centuries?"

"I don't know," he whispers. "But I don't think we'd have met if we weren't meant to."

I wonder if he's right. Part of me thinks the universe is only showing me what I'm missing so it can yank it away from me. I could start spiraling fast if I'm not careful, but Cole doesn't give me the chance. He tips my head back and kisses a small trail down my neck. My body tingles, and I arch into his touch.

"You are the most beautiful woman I have ever seen," he whispers against the hollow of my throat.

I wrap my legs around his waist, pulling him into me. My arms encircle his neck, and my hands wind into his hair. He kisses up the side of my neck and at the underside of my chin. He stops for a second to look at me, and I nearly gasp. His eyes are deep, dark, and endless in a way I've never seen before. His desire is palpable.

His hands slide into my hair, and he pulls me to him. The first kiss is soft. The second is a little more insistent. The third is explosive.

Our tongues explore, and my hips undulate. Cole lets out a deep moan, and I feel the vibration throughout my body.

He reaches down, hooking his arm under my knee and lifting my leg. His hand slides down my thigh to the edge of my panties. He curls a finger under the elastic and looks into my eyes; a silent question passes between us. I nod for him to continue, and he wastes no time. The tentative finger that was toying with the edge of my underwear is replaced with his hand fisting the fabric. He tugs it off of me, letting it fall to the floor.

His mouth curves as he watches it land. "This floor is definitely clean enough to eat off of, but so is the counter."

He works the bottom of my dress up until it reaches my hips, and I'm laid bare to him. He kneels before me and rests his hands on the inside of my thighs, carefully pushing my legs aside. I keep my eyes fixed on him as he slowly kisses his way from my knee to the inside of my thigh, nearly reaching the spot I crave before pulling back and starting over again with the other knee.

I'm nearly panting when he reaches my center. He doesn't stop this time. My eyelids flutter closed as his mouth makes contact. His tongue swirls, and his mouth sucks, and I wonder where he learned how to do this. I'm moaning, my hips are bucking, and I can't even feel embarrassed about it. Cole alternates his technique, adding pressure and speed, and it isn't long before my back is arching, and I'm crying out and seeing stars explode behind my eyelids.

When he finishes, he stands slowly as I sit up, resting on my elbows. There's a look of reverence on his face that stuns me. He's staring at me as if I'm a work of art to be revered and studied. He leans in, taking my face in his hands.

"Where did you come from?" he whispers.

I smile. "I could ask you the same thing."

I part my legs farther, needing him closer. He obliges, and I feel him firm and ready, pressing against me. Feeling brazen, I reach out and undo his belt and unfasten the button on his pants. I push the zipper down, never taking my eyes off of him. He tips his head. It's a silent plea for me to continue. I unclip his suspenders and slide my hands into the waistband of his pants, shoving them down and taking his underwear with it. He stands in front of me, looking more like a god than a man.

I wrap my hand around him, and he gasps, leaning into my touch. My entire body aches to have him as close as possible. Anticipation builds in my chest, and a slight hesitation enters my thoughts. Once we do this, there's no going back. And yet, I'll have to go back. Back to my century while he stays in his. The thought threatens to undo this moment, and I push it away, unwilling to give up any of this experience until I absolutely have to. Whatever comes will come, but for now, I'm here with this man, and I know I'm exactly where I'm meant to be.

I guide him toward me, and then it's his turn to hesitate. "I don't have—"

I press a finger to his lips. "Shh. I've got it covered." He squints, and I remember what year we're in. "Where I'm from, there are pills a woman can take, and all you need to know is I'm taking them."

He seems to consider what I've said, and then he moves

close, the tip of him presses against me. I shift my hips and hook my legs around him, bringing him in. We freeze, taking in the sensation. Staring into each other's eyes, we don't say anything, and yet we say everything. We start to move together. It's slow and deliberate as we pace ourselves. We don't know if we'll have this opportunity again, and want to make it last.

My body vibrates with need, and he reads my unspoken cue, positioning his body so he meets me where I need him. With each thrust of his hips, he hits the spot that's screaming for him. And then I'm screaming for him as he moves faster and harder. We grunt and groan, and with a final gasp, we collide—our satiated bodies resting against each other.

Our breaths are ragged but slowly begin to even out. The low trumpet and soft piano flow from the crackling speaker. A man croons about the woman he loves, and I think I know what he means. That both terrifies and excites me.

"Sylvie," Cole murmurs against my shoulder. He pushes up, meeting my eyes. "I don't have words, but also, I have so many."

I chuckle softly. "I can relate."

He looks around like he doesn't remember where we are. "I am so sorry. You must think I'm an animal."

I frown. "Why would I think that? I mean, you are," I say, nudging his knee with mine. "But you say it like it's a bad thing."

"You deserve more than a counter in this damn cafe. I got too carried away."

"Uh-uh. We were both carried away. And I think the setting is perfect."

"You do?"

"Absolutely," I say, nodding. "This is where it all began for us, Cole. I can't think of a more appropriate place for us to, well, you know."

A wry smile fills his face. "For us to what?"

"Cole," I playfully warn.

"You mean, for us to fuck like our lives depended on it?"

I giggle. "Yeah, that's exactly what I meant."

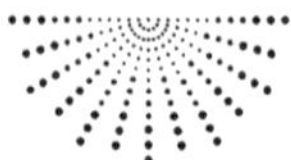

"Well, well, well, looks like someone had a good time yesterday," Mel chirps from behind her desk.

"What makes you say that?"

She shakes her head, pointing at me. "Oh, come on. You have the biggest grin on your face! I saw it the minute you rounded the corner."

"Wait, you were watching from the window?"

"Hell, yeah, I was! I knew you were spending the day with your mystery man, and you never responded to my texts last night." She glares at me.

"Sorry," I say, grimacing. "It was kind of a late night."

"Uh-huh, I figured as much and I need details, lady."

"Um, well, it was a nice night."

"How nice?" she asks, cocking her head.

I bite my lip. "*Really* nice."

"Oh, shit! Look at you! I'm so happy for you, Sylvie. It's about time you got some."

"Shh!" I press a finger to my lips. "Will you please be

quiet? The whole office doesn't need to hear about my escapades."

"You mean your 'sexcapades.'" She falls into a fit of laughter, and I join in. I can't help myself.

Waltzing into my office, I sit at my desk, intent on starting my day. A half hour passes, and I'm still staring at the sign-in screen. My thoughts are heavy and full of Cole.

After our, um, activities, Cole insisted we go back to his house. He made us grilled cheese sandwiches and tomato soup. We ate at his tiny kitchen table, and for a short time, I allowed myself to imagine what it would be like if I lived there.

We would spend our days working in the cafe and our nights in our cozy little home. It would be so simple and so perfect.

When we finished eating, we went up to Cole's room. I had hoped we might have a repeat of earlier, but after stripping down to our underwear, Cole just wanted to hold me in his arms. We lay together, absorbing the moment, both of us lost in thought. At some point, I fell asleep, and when I woke up, his arms were still wrapped around me. He was looking at me like he was trying to memorize my face.

We shared a kiss, and then I had to head home and get ready for work. We parted at the cafe door. Even though I saw him this morning, it feels strange to not have my first coffee with him.

My morning progresses, and eventually, I'm able to focus and get a little work done. Mel pokes her head into my office around noon. "Hey, you."

"Hey, yourself. How're things out there?"

"Eh," she says with a shrug. "Kind of boring. Not nearly as exciting as your activities last night." She waggles her eyebrows.

"Will you stop?" I say, laughing.

"Never." She makes it like she's going to leave, but then she pops back in. "Oh! I almost forgot. Curtis is taking me out for dinner on Friday."

"Curtis?"

She flaps her hand. "I've mentioned him. At least I think I have," she says, tapping a manicured nail against her lip. "Anyway, he's the one. I'm sure of it."

I cock my head and arc my brow, never uttering a word.

"Oh, shut up. Listen. I know I'm always saying that."

"You are," I agree, nodding.

"Whatever. This time it's different, and before you go asking how, it just is. I can feel it. Okay?" Her eyes are earnest and hopeful.

I smile. "Okay."

"Okay? Really?"

"If you feel it, then I believe it. I mean, his name begins with the right letter, so how bad can he be?"

Mel giggles. "Right? That's what I said. It's like your guy, too. Guess we both have a thing for *C* men."

"Oh my God," I say, covering my face with my hand. "Don't call it that."

She seems to consider it for a beat before dissolving in laughter. I quickly follow.

"Well, Mel," I say, wiping my eyes and trying to catch my breath. "You know what this means right? It means it must be fate." I wink at her.

She smiles widely. "True, true! Thank you for always being so supportive." She snaps her fingers. "Hey, what do you say we plan a double date?"

My mouth loses every bit of moisture, and my palms begin to sweat. "A double date?"

"Yeah! I'm dying to meet this guy and besides, all that

time alone with Curtis is probably not the best idea for me. I'm so weak around him and I'm trying to play it cool." She winces.

"Um, yeah. I'll, uh, check with Cole and get back to you."

"Awesome," she says, tapping the doorframe before heading back to her desk.

"Shit," I mutter. I knew I'd eventually have to explain my little secret. I guess I just thought I'd have more time.

I HAVEN'T SEEN Cole since leaving the cafe yesterday morning. I thought about ducking out early yesterday to catch him before he closed for the day, but fucking Jackie was lurking around my office. The last thing I wanted to do was give her another thing to try to hold over my head.

I tug open the door, and my eyes ping-pong around the cafe in search of him. He comes rushing out of the kitchen a moment later. When he spots me, he hops over the counter and strides across the room.

"There you are." He grabs my face, pulling my mouth to his. This is not our typical hello, but it's one I could get used to.

We pull apart reluctantly. My face flushes as I breathlessly whisper, "Here I am."

He tucks a lock of hair behind my ear. "I've missed you."

I give a cursory glance around the cafe. I know we're alone, but I still feel like we're on display.

Cole places a finger under my chin, turning me to face him. "You're not suddenly shy on me, are you?"

"No, no, I, just, um …"

He laughs, and my mouth twists. "It's okay. I know this is all so new, and maybe I shouldn't be so forward. But I just can't help myself with you. When you're here, I want to be near you, and when you're gone, I long for you to be here." He shrugs, looking vulnerable.

I rest my palm on his cheek. "I know the feeling." My voice is low and husky.

A throat clears behind us. I jolt away from Cole, but he doesn't seem to share my alarm. He casually turns, grinning at his mom. "Hi-ya, Ma. You remember Sylvie?"

"Remember? Pssh, you haven't stopped jabbering on about her since you met." She tilts her head, locking eyes with me. A sweet smile fills her face. "It's really lovely to see you, Sylvie. I ought to thank you while I'm at it."

"Thank me?"

"Why, of course. You're the reason my boy has had such a spring in his step as of late. It's been wonderful to see him excited about something other than this old cafe." She winks at Cole.

"Old, huh? Well, maybe it's time to modernize things." He taps the pad of his finger against his chin. "Actually," he says, jutting the same finger in the air. "Sylvie here had an ingenious idea the other night."

My face pinches. What is he talking about? "I did?"

"Oh, now, come on. Don't be modest. You remember." When I don't say anything, he prods on. "That thing about eating off the fl—"

I let out a laugh loud enough to cover up the word. "Let's not bore your poor mom with our crazy ideas."

"Hmm," Cole's mom hums, her eyes zinging between us. She looks as though she's on the verge of asking what we're talking about, but with a slight shake of her head, she seems to think better of it. "Listen, Cole, I'm sorry to spring this on you with such short notice, but I'm afraid I can't stay to help you with the morning rush today."

"Everything all right?" Cole asks.

"Well, I hope so. Greta Kingston stopped by this morning. Seems her wrist has been giving her some trouble. She's going to see Doc Sterling this morning and asked me to come with her. You know how she is. Gets herself all worked up and can't focus. Poor thing."

"It's nice of you to accompany her."

"I just feel bad for leaving you in a lurch is all," she says, wringing her hands.

"Nonsense. I'll be just fine. In fact," he says, turning to me with a crooked grin, "Sylvie will help."

"I will?" I swear all I'm doing is parroting their words back to them, but they keep catching me off guard. It's like I've been thrust into a game of tennis, but my opponents are experts, and I barely know how to hold a racket.

Cole leans in, keeping his voice low enough that his mom won't hear. "It's okay if you can't stay. I know you have work. I just thought it might be fun to spend the day together."

How can I say no to that? The answer is I can't. "I have a lot of unused vacation days that Mel is always trying to get me to take. Let me hop outside and call the office quick."

The grin on his face is so wide it makes the corners of his eyes crinkle.

"It was nice seeing you again," I call to Cole's mom. "I'm just going to pop outside for a moment, but I'll be back to help Cole." I steal a quick glance at him. My stomach does a somersault when I find him looking back at me.

Outside, the sidewalk is bustling with activity; I nearly collide with a woman pushing a posh-looking stroller with an equally posh-looking toy poodle blanketed inside. The woman glares at me, and I swear her little dog does, too. I mutter an apology and take a step back, leaning against the mottled brick exterior. With my phone in hand, I dial Mel's number. She answers on the second ring.

"Hey, Mel. You know those personal days you keep begging me to take?"

"Uh-huh," she says, drawing out the "huh."

"Well, I'm taking one. Today, actually."

"Woo-hoo! That's my girl!"

CHAPTER TWENTY

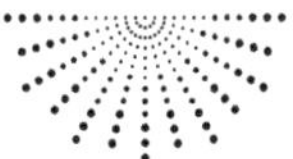

It's amazing what a difference an hour makes. When I first walked into the cafe this morning, it was empty, and now it's filled with sounds of clinking glasses, scraping forks, and murmured conversations.

"Can I top off your coffee for you, Mr. Wilcox?"

The surly man twists the ends of his graying mustache in contemplation. It's not a question that should take much thought to answer, but I've noticed no one here moves with any sense of urgency.

Mr. Wilcox clears his throat and peers up at me through thick lenses. "Yes, I believe that would be nice. Thank you, dear."

With a nod and a smile, I pour a stream of coffee from my pot, watching as it nearly reaches the brim of his cup. I'm new at this, but I learned quickly that it's important to always save room for cream. Years of drinking fancy lattes and cappuccinos have left me a little clueless about the fine art of drip coffee.

I move around the cafe, offering coffee and chatting up the customers. Every so often, I glance toward the counter, catching Cole's watchful eyes always trained on me, the faintest hint of pride on his face, and something else. Something like hope? I know because I feel it too, though I keep reminding myself that this … all of this, is temporary. As much as we might wish it could be permanent, there's nothing either of us can do to change the situation.

I'm not from here. And not in the simple sense of I'm from a different state or even a different time zone. I'm from an entirely different century.

Once I've made the rounds, I breeze toward Cole, setting the empty coffee pot on the counter. He grins at me. "You're a natural, you know that? You have a way with people."

My face scrunches. "I do?"

He nods. "Just look around. Everyone has a contented look on their face. Even miserly Mr. Wilcox over there. In fact, I think you might've managed to coax a bit of a smile out of him. A rare feat, indeed."

I laugh. "I'm just being kind, is all. There's nothing special about it."

"On the contrary. Everything about you is special."

Our eyes meet, and it's as if we're two sides of a flame, burning bright and hot. Most flames extinguish eventually, but it's hard to imagine that happening with us.

Still, feeling the heaviness of the moment, I'm the first to break the stare, peering out into the busy cafe. Though I don't see a single face besides Cole's. I don't have to look at him. I see him clearly wherever I look.

You're gonna get your heart broken, Sylvie.

The thought swirls around my mind like a spoon stirring coffee, but I can't bring myself to care.

An hour later, the cafe is nearly empty. I'm busy wiping up a table against the wall while Cole repositions chairs, pushing them until their backs reach the edge of the table.

"Have you told anyone about us?" The question sounds casual on my tongue, though it's anything but.

He stands tall, scratching his chin. "I'm not sure I know what you mean. My mom knows, of course."

"Yeah, I know that, but I'm talking about other people. Friends or even acquaintances?"

He rubs his jaw. "I don't really have many friends these days. The cafe has kept me pretty busy. Aside from the regulars, I really only talk to my mom. And you, of course." He winks.

I feel my cheeks warm. "Would you tell anyone? That is, if there *was* someone to tell?"

He nods without pause. "Absolutely."

"Hmm." I look down at the table I've been wiping over and over. It's definitely clean now.

"Any particular reason you're asking?"

I lift my hand off the rag and give it a swipe along the apron tied around my waist. "Um," I cross my arms over my chest and lean back against the wall. "Like you, I don't really have many friends, but I do have one. Mel. She's my assistant at work and also my best friend."

He tips his head, wordlessly urging me to continue.

"She knows about you, but not *all* about you."

"All as in …?" He arcs a brow.

"As in, you live in the 1930s. No big deal." I chuckle, though I feel my stomach tightening. It *is* a big deal. The biggest deal.

"I see. Do you want to tell her?"

"Well, it's more of a need and less of a want, actually."

"How so?" He rests a hand on his hip, and my eyes zero in on the flex of his forearm muscles.

Focus, Sylvie.

"She wants to go on a double date with us and it's kind of forced my hand. I could lie and tell her you're busy, but that would only buy me a little time. She'll keep asking and besides, I don't want to lie. Not to her."

He smiles. "So don't lie."

"That's your grand advice? I should just call her up and say, 'Hey, Mel, remember that guy I told you about? Well, turns out he lives in a totally different century and I have to time travel to hang out with him.'"

I smirk, but he just shrugs. "Why not?"

My eyes widen. "You're serious?"

"Sure. If she's as good of a friend as you say she is, then you should tell her."

"And how do you propose I do that?"

"Call her and have her meet you outside."

"Then what?"

"Then you take her by the hand and lead her inside." He says it like it's so simple. And maybe it is.

My eyes flit around the cafe as I let his idea take root. "But what if it—"

Cole shakes his head. "Uh-uh, we'll worry about that *if* it happens."

"I guess it's worth a shot," I say, finally.

"It is. Trust me." He watches me carefully. "Go on," he says, tipping his head toward the door.

"What? Now?"

"Now is as good a time as any. Besides, no one else is here at the moment."

"So, if she freaks out, she can do it in private." I grin.

"Precisely."

CHAPTER TWENTY-ONE

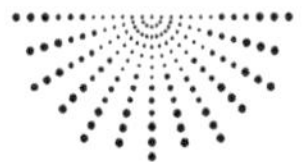

I have no clue if this will even work, but it's like Cole said. It's worth a shot. I can't continue with things like they've been—only telling Mel part of the story. It feels like a lie, and it pretty much is. I've told her everything, but the most important detail. And now, as I see her rushing down the sidewalk toward me, I feel my stomach start to churn. "Here goes nothing," I mutter.

"Hey, lady!" Mel's smile is grand, though she looks a little confused. "Why are we meeting here, exactly?" She eyes the building, and it's clear she doesn't see what I see.

Suddenly, I'm feeling more unsure of this plan but also stuck. There's no turning back now.

"I wanted to introduce you to Cole," I say, my voice shaking, betraying me.

"O-kay," she says slowly. "Is he meeting us here?"

"Not exactly. He's already here. You just can't see him."

She bites at her lip and looks down at the dirty sidewalk.

"It's not what you think." I rush the words, hoping to quell the worry I can see etched on her forehead.

Her eyes snap to mine, and that same look of hope I saw

in Cole's earlier passes between us. "All righty," she says, smoothing her hands over her coat. "If I can't see him, then where is he?"

I tilt my head toward the cafe door, though if she sees things the way they are on Google Maps, then to her, it's just a boarded-up entrance. "Um, in there?" It comes out like a question, making her eyes widen. I clear my throat and try again. "He's just inside. Come on. I'll show you." I grab her hand and tug her along with me, giving her no time to protest.

I turn the knob and push the door open the same way I always do, only this time, I feel Mel's hand in mine. Her fingers tighten as I take us through the opening. On the other side, Cole stands in the center of the cafe, ready to greet us. I start to smile, but it freezes partway on my face when I realize Mel's hand is no longer in mine. I wiggle my fingers, slowly lifting them in front of my face.

I let my hand fall to my side. "It didn't work."

Cole takes a few steps toward me until we're standing toe to toe. Placing a finger under my chin, he tilts my head until our eyes meet. "Hey," he whispers. "We knew there was a chance it wouldn't work, but at least you tried."

I swallow around the lump in my throat. Mel is my best friend and the only person in the world I wanted Cole to meet. Without their introduction, none of this feels real.

"Tell me what you're thinking."

I let out a breath. "I just really wanted the two of you to know each other."

He presses his lips into a firm line and nods. A moment later, his eyes widen, and he spins on his heel, dashing behind the counter.

"What are you doing?"

He holds up a finger while he shuffles things around on a shelf with his other hand. "There it is," he declares, slapping a notepad and pen on top of the counter. He uncaps the pen and begins furiously scribbling on the paper.

I take a few steps toward him until the page comes into view. The words "Dear Mel" stop me in my tracks. "You're writing her a letter?"

He looks up. "I am. You said you wanted us to meet and if we can't do it in person, then we can do it this way. Think of it like we're pen pals." He gets back to writing, and a few minutes later, the letter is folded and slid into an envelope. Cole seals it and writes Mel's name in big block letters across the front.

"Here," he says, handing me the envelope. "I'm sure your friend is really confused right about now and definitely concerned. Take this and go alleviate her worry."

I hold the letter against my chest and open my mouth to say, well, I'm not sure what I can say besides, "Thank you."

Cole smiles warmly. "Go on, now. I'll leave the door unlocked so you can come back later and tell me how it goes." He gives me a wink and tips his head toward the door.

Wordlessly, I take the knob in my hand, and with a quick turn, I'm back out on the sidewalk. Mel is pacing back and forth but stops suddenly when she sees me. Rushing toward me, she grips my arms, and her eyes begin assessing every inch of me. "Sylvie, what the fuck?" She releases my arms and presses a palm to her forehead, letting it glide down her face. "You were holding my hand and taking me, I don't even know where and then you were just gone. Where the hell did you go?"

I suck in a breath like the air will give me the courage to explain myself. It doesn't work, but I press on anyway. "Mel, listen, this is super bizarre. I know that. Trust me. But when I walked through that door," I say, arcing a thumb behind me, "I walked into Cole's Cafe."

Mel shakes her head. "I don't understand. Sylvie, there is

no cafe." Her voice is quiet and even, like she's afraid to say the wrong thing.

I give her a sympathetic smile. "You're right. There isn't a cafe. Not now, anyway. But there was. It was here in the 1930s and it was perfect." I turn to look at the building I just exited. The sign above the door is so clear to me, but I know my friend can't see it, and it breaks my heart a little, and it makes me feel special, like I'm in on a secret.

"Wait a minute, your guy, his name is Cole, right?"

"Yep." I nod, never taking my eyes off the cafe.

"Oh, Sylvie. You don't think …"

The pain in her voice grips me, and I spin around to find sad, sullen eyes watching me carefully. "It's all right, Mel. I know how all of this sounds, but look," I say, holding up the envelope from Cole. It was white and crisp moments ago, but now, as I stand here in front of Mel, it's yellowed with age and brittle from time. It shocks me, though it shouldn't. It was written in 1934, nearly a hundred years ago.

"What's this?"

I swallow the emotion in my throat. "It's from Cole. He wrote it for you."

CHAPTER TWENTY-TWO

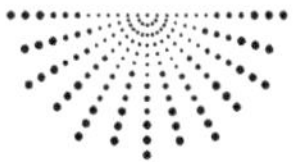

"So, let me get this straight. That old dilapidated building is like a teleport to the 1930s?"

"Yeah, something like that. Although, it seems I'm the only one capable of being teleported." I reach for my tea and lean back against the cushion as I sip.

Mel and I moved the conversation back to my apartment and away from curious ears on the street. I made us some tea while I explained the situation as best as I could. She read her letter from Cole and it seemed to change things somehow. It convinced her in a way I was struggling to do. I have no idea what was in the letter. She didn't offer it to me, and I didn't ask to read it, though I'm dying to. I'll ask Cole later when I go back to the cafe.

"This is wild, Sylvie." Mel pushes up to her feet and begins pacing around my tiny apartment. "I mean, do you even know what this means?"

I shake my head. "Not a clue."

She stops mid-step and pivots toward me. "It means you found a portal, or maybe you are the portal. Either way, you managed to locate a blip in the space-time continuum. This is wild."

"You said that already, Doc Brown. I think you've been watching too much *Back to the Future*."

"Are you kidding? I don't think you've been watching enough."

I chuckle, but she doesn't. Scrubbing a hand through her hair, she strides over to the window, peering out like there might be answers to glean from the gray clouds taking up residence in the sky.

"How did this happen?" Her voice is just above a whisper.

"It's like I told you. I got splashed by a car and needed to clean up the mess. The cafe was just … there. I never even thought for a second that I was traveling back in time until it basically slapped me in the face."

She turns around to face me. "Do you love him?" She shakes her head, not waiting for an answer. "Of course, you do. And why wouldn't you?" She crosses the room and takes a seat next to me. "Leave it to you to find the perfect man who just so happens to be living in a different century."

I sigh. "Leave it to me, is right."

"So, what are you going to do?"

It's a question I've asked myself over and over, though every time, I try to push it out of my mind because it scares me. I don't have an answer, and I don't even think there is one. I swallow past the lump in my throat. "I honestly don't know."

COLE HAS BEEN patient with me since I came back to the cafe after talking to Mel. He's not pressing me for details, even though I'm sure he'd love them. He can tell I'm lost in my thoughts, so he's giving me a little space. He ushered me over to a quiet little table in the corner of the cafe and left me with a slice of pie while he went about cleaning up behind the counter. It's odd sitting over here when I'm used to being perched on one of the stools lining the long counter.

I watch as Cole busies himself, scrubbing the sides of the old coffee maker and wiping down the steel workspace. He's meticulous and careful, and I love him. It's not even something to consider. It's just something I know, like the way I know my name. It's a part of me. And when Mel asked me, she knew it, too.

I've always thought love was this powerful thing. Like it had magical powers or something, and considering I found it by time traveling, maybe it does. Cole and I exist on two totally different plains, and yet we somehow meet in the middle.

"Penny for your thoughts?"

"Hmm?" I peer up in a daze, my eyes taking a moment to focus on the man in front of me.

Cole presses both palms to the table and leans in. "You've been in your own world over here and it's okay. Take all the time you need. But I just wanted to check in and make sure you're okay. You haven't said much since you got here."

"Am I okay?" I let out a long sigh. "That's the question of the hour, isn't it?"

His face scrunches. "Did something happen with Mel?"

I chuckle, but there's no humor in it. "Have a seat," I say, tipping my head toward the empty chair across from me.

Cole sits, scooting closer to me. He rests his hands on the table next to mine. His fingers splay out, not touching mine, though I sense they're itching to.

"I needed to tell Mel. I know that, but I also knew that it would change things once I did."

"Change things how?"

I pinch my lower lip between two fingers and lightly tug,

taking a moment to assemble my thoughts into words. "There was us *before* Mel and now there's us *after* Mel. Before, we were in our own little bubble. It was just us in this safe little corner. But the thing about bubbles is—"

"They pop." Cole smiles sadly.

I nod. "They do. And, well, I guess Mel popped the bubble because now I have all of these other thoughts in my head. Intrusive thoughts I had managed to keep at bay before. Thoughts like, what will happen to us? Where do we go from here? How can we continue like this when I live in one century and you live in another? You know, little things like that." I chuckle without humor.

Cole presses his lips together. "I've had those thoughts, too."

"You have?"

"Of course, but I'm afraid I don't have any answers."

"Yeah," I whisper. "Neither do I."

He stretches his fingers, hooking my pinky with his. "Then let's not spoil this night trying to find them."

"But what happens if—"

He presses a finger against my lips. "Shh. We can't worry about *then* when all we have is *now*."

I close my eyes, still feeling the warmth of his skin against my mouth. It's real. Even if it doesn't make sense. It's real, and it's happening, and he's right. We don't know how long we have, so we shouldn't waste time worrying about what might be coming.

"Listen," he coos. "Do you hear that?"

I still my movements and focus on the soft crooning wafting out of the little radio.

"They're playing our song. And you know what that means, don't you?" Cole stands, holding out his hand.

I take his hand and try to memorize how it feels in mine. Rough and warm. He pulls me to my feet and guides me wordlessly to the center of the cafe. Instinct takes over. We sway and spin and soak up the moment. Cole called this "our song," but he didn't mean it literally. It isn't just one song that's ours. It's all of them. Every single sweet melody that pours from that old cafe radio plays for us and us alone.

I rest my cheek against his shoulder and slide my face along the smooth lines of his crisp white shirt. Pulling back, I gaze up at him and find him looking down at me. We stare at one another, both of us wondering how we could simultaneously be so lucky and unlucky. And then, as if we both feel the need to chase the bad thoughts away, we lean toward each other. Me on my tiptoes and him curving his neck. Our mouths meet in the middle. Lips press together and slowly part.

We kiss like all we have is this moment, and that may very well be true. Cole grips the sides of my face with his hands, pulling me even closer. We kiss with fervor, with the kind of wild abandon I've only ever read about.

When we pull apart, we're breathless. Our chests heave, and our eyes scan each other's. Cole looks over my shoulder at the table behind us and then back at me. Reading his mind, I give him a nod. He steps swiftly toward it, and with one sweep of his arm, he sends the salt and pepper shaker and the little dish of sugar cubes flying across the cafe. I watch as the lid springs from the pepper and ping-pongs across the floor, speckling the gray linoleum with bits of black. My eyes widen.

Cole clears his throat, and when I glance back at him, he looks possessed. His nostrils flare, and his eyes are nearly black. He crooks a finger, beckoning me to him. I don't hesitate. When I'm close enough, he wraps an arm around my waist while his free hand grips my throat like a necklace. My whole body flushes with heat. A small whimper escapes my mouth, and a feral growl escapes his.

We crash into each other—a full-force collision without any regard for the impact. Cole spins us around. I feel the table as it presses against my backside. His fingers move to my waist and slide up, taking my shirt along with them. He lifts it up and over my head, tossing it somewhere on the peppered floor. He glides me back until I'm laid flat. The smooth wood is cool on my skin.

His mouth explores my neck, moving down over the swell of my breasts. He flicks each nipple with his tongue, and I feel the sensation much lower. My hips rock and he grins. "Impatient little thing, aren't you?"

He continues moving down my body, taking his time despite my moans of protest. He hooks his fingers into the waistband of my skirt, tugging it down my legs, and then he presses a kiss to my center with nothing but my underwear between us. It's too much and not enough at the same time. Again, my hips move, trying to get the friction I so desperately need.

I feel the warmth of his breath on my skin, and when I peel my eyes open, I find him looking up at me. "No matter what happens, I will never forget your face at this moment."

Keeping his gaze locked on mine, he bites the edge of my underwear. Taking the fabric between his teeth, he slowly glides it off of me. It's the single hottest moment of my entire life.

Nothing is tentative after that. He takes me in his mouth, sucking and licking as I writhe on the little cafe table. My moans drown out the soft music, creating a new soundtrack.

As soon as I begin to plateau, he thrusts inside of me. I gasp and my body jackknifes. He grips my hair in his fist, and I press my mouth to his, sucking on his lower lip. He grunts as he pounds into me like he's starving and I'm his only meal. I feel that familiar sensation as it begins to build inside of me, and my body starts to vibrate. We move faster, each of us chasing the feeling we so desperately need. I get there first, panting and moaning, and with a primal growl, Cole joins me.

Our bodies are slick as we slowly lower back onto the small table. I'm amazed it was able to withstand the assault we just gave it. For a moment, the only sound is our labored breaths and the soft music flowing from the old radio.

Cole hovers over me, propping himself up on his forearms. "I will suffer through a lifetime of *thens* for every *now* I have with you." He leans down, kissing me sweetly.

I close my eyes and a few tears escape. When the time comes—and I know it's coming—I don't know how I'll ever be able to say goodbye.

CHAPTER TWENTY-THREE

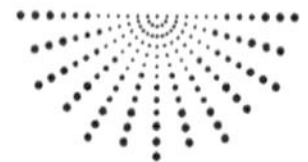

"Morning, Mel," I say as I stride into the room.

"Good morning to you. And how are things in 1934?" She grins mischievously.

"Shh," I chide. "What if someone hears you?"

She flaps her hand. "Pssh. What if? No one would even have a clue what we're talking about."

I nod. "I guess you're right." Looking down at the brown tweed carpet, I let out a sigh.

"Uh-oh. That doesn't sound good. What happened?" Mel leans in and then starts shaking her head. "No, we're not having this conversation here like this." She walks around her desk, taking my hand in hers and tugging us toward my corner office. "Come on." Once we reach the door, she tips her chin toward the two cushy high-back chairs against the wall. "Go have a seat. I'll be right back."

I stumble into the room, letting my purse fall from my shoulder. Taking off my jacket, I fling it onto my desk and slump into the cozy chair. I lean forward, shoulders on my knees and my head in my hands.

"Shit," Mel tsks as soon as she spots me from the doorway. "This is worse than I thought. Here." She thrusts a steaming cup into my hands. "It's not Cole's coffee, but it's strong, and I may have overdone it with the sugar. What else is new?"

I take the cup, wrapping both hands around it. The warmth reminds me of Cole and the way his hands feel in mine. My eyes begin to well. I try to blink away the tears, but one escapes.

"Hey," Mel coos, leaning in. "Talk to me."

"He's perfect, Mel. As in, perfect in every way I need him to be. When I'm with him, I can see things I never pictured before. Like, how incredible our lives could be together. And it's just simple, you know? There's nothing complicated about us. There are no climbing corporate ladders or vying for the next promotion. It's just him and me and that sweet little cafe."

She nods, smiling sadly. "That all sounds wonderful."

"It is. There's just this one teeny tiny little problem. I live in 2023 and he lives in 1934. And no matter how much I try to ignore that, it's reality. I don't know how to get around it. We were doomed right from the start."

Mel rests a hand on my knee, giving it a light squeeze. "That may be so, but answer me this. If you had it to do all over again, would you?"

"Without hesitation," I say, head bobbing vigorously.

"Well, there you go. No matter how it ends, it was worth it. I think that tells you everything you need to know."

"But," I huff. "Where do we go from here?"

"Why do you have to go anywhere?"

My face scrunches. "Well, I mean, this isn't just a little obstacle for us to get past, Mel. Cole and I, we live in different centuries."

She grins. "Yes, I know, but so what? Sure, things may

come to an end eventually, but eventually isn't now. So, why dwell on it?"

I bite my lip, staring off toward the big windows of my office. Is she right? Should I even be worrying about this right now? "You sound just like Cole," I say.

"He's a smart man. You should listen to him. Listen to us, Sylvie," Mel continues. "If you waste all the time you have with Cole worrying about when and how it might end, you're going to regret that more than anything else."

Shit. She's right. I rest my hand on top of hers. "How do you know so much?"

She shrugs. "I have the advantage of being a little removed from the situation. Sometimes you can't see things clearly when you're too close."

She gives my hand a squeeze and rises slowly from the chair. "Oh," she says as she reaches the door. "I almost forgot. Allison wants to meet with you before lunch to finalize the budget for the strip mall project."

"Ugh," I groan. "Didn't we already have that meeting?"

Mel chuckles. "You did, but you know Allison. She's nothing if not thorough."

I nod, rolling my eyes. "It's probably for the best. I could use the distraction. What time did you say the meeting was?"

"I didn't," she says, with a gleam in her eye. "It's at eleven."

I glance at the clock. It's already after nine. "Well, I guess I better get my shit together then, huh?"

"In more ways than one." She gives me a pointed look and then disappears out into the hallway.

The rest of my morning is a blur of numbers and paperwork. At ten minutes to eleven, I'm printing out my final report. "Wish me luck," I say to Mel as I breeze past her desk.

"I would, but you don't need it," she calls after me.

I smile. She always has my back. Even when I have no clue what I'm doing. That's not the case here, though. I could do this job in my sleep. I used to think that was a flex, but now I'm not so sure.

"Knock, knock," I say as I rap my knuckles against Allison's partially open door.

"Ah, Sylvie, come in, come in. Have a seat." She gestures to the chair across from her. Placing her elbows on her desk, she steeples her hands under her chin. "Have you got those numbers for me?"

I nod, passing the report over to her. She flips through the pages as a smile begins to bloom on her face. It's small at first but grows into a full grin by the time she reaches the end of the report. "Excellent work, as usual. I can always count on you to come through for me."

"It's no trouble at all, really." No truer words have ever been said. I've filled out forms at the doctor's office that took me longer.

She smiles warmly. "I'm so anxious to get started on this. Did you hear? We break ground in two weeks! We were just waiting on these final numbers and they are right where they need to be, so it's full steam ahead."

"That's exciting. Did you tell me where this new strip mall is going? I can't remember if I knew the address or not. It's just been all numbers for me," I say, chuckling.

"Oh, sure. It's actually pretty close by. Over on Wellington and State. You know those old dilapidated buildings that are such an eyesore?"

If you were wondering if it was possible to feel your heart travel through your chest and up into your throat, it is. I swear I can hear the beating in my neck, and if I place a hand there, I'll feel the steady thrum as it picks up its pace. I know those "old dilapidated buildings" well. One in particular. But I must've heard her wrong. "Wait, Allison, you don't mean the place on the corner, do you?"

"Uh-huh, that's exactly where I mean."

I suck in a breath, trying to steady my heart. "But aren't they protected? I mean, they've been around for so long. They must be a historical site."

She chuckles. "You sound just like that guy on the city council. They are old, but not historic. In fact, they are probably close to falling down on their own at this point. They've become a hazard. We were originally going to try to preserve the structure, but it's proven to be too costly. Bulldozing is set for Wednesday, two weeks from now."

"B-bulldozing?" I stammer.

"Yep! Isn't that great? It's going to breathe new life into that tired old corner."

New life. There's already life there. Beautiful, simple life. Except, I'm the only one that knows about it. I need to get out of here. I have to go to Cole. Warn him. Be with him. Love him. This looming deadline I've been feeling has been set. Our time is running out.

I manage to find some semblance of strength and say my goodbyes to Allison. She grins widely at me, none the wiser. She has no idea about the turmoil that's going on inside me.

I rush down the hall, practically sprinting.

"Whoa! What's going on?" Mel springs from her seat, worry etched on her face.

"It's happening, Mel."

"What's happening?"

"Eventually. It's here. It's now."

CHAPTER TWENTY-FOUR

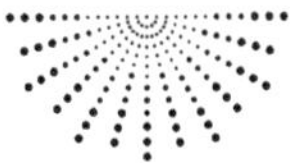

"Cole," I call out as I burst through the door. The little bell clangs as it slams against the wood. I spin my head in every direction before spotting him by the coffee maker.

He turns to greet me, a carefree smile on his face. But once he sees me, all traces of humor are gone. His eyes widen, and his brow furrows. "Sylvie? What is it? What's wrong?" The coffee mug in his hands bangs on the counter as he sets it down hard. He lifts himself onto the counter, gliding over it with ease, and races toward me. I'm reminded of the last time he did that. He couldn't get to me fast enough. That day, I felt wanted and desired more than I ever had in my life. Now, as I stand here, ready to tell him the worst news he would ever hear, I find myself wishing I could go back to that day. Back when all we had were beautiful, simple moments.

He takes my hands in his, squeezing them. "Talk to me."

"You know that thing we didn't want to talk about? The one where all of this would end?"

He nods, his mouth a grim line.

"It's probably time for us to talk about it." I close my eyes, and a lone tear trickles down my cheek.

Cole catches it with his finger. "Come, have a seat." He leads me to one of the empty round tables in the center of the cafe.

I drop into the chair, feeling more defeated than ever. Cole sits beside me. The second our eyes meet, I start talking, and I don't stop until I tell him everything. All about the strip mall and the demolition date. Somehow, I manage to say it all without crying, but once I finish, the tears come, and I don't think they'll ever stop.

Cole wraps his arms around me. "It's okay," he whispers.

I want to ask him how he can say that. Does he know something I don't? Because from where I'm standing, nothing is okay and it never will be again.

COLE SAYS that pie fixes everything. I don't think it can fix this problem, but it dulls the edge a bit. Though it also makes it sharper. Because in two weeks, simple pleasures like this, where I'm sitting on my favorite orange stool, eating a piece of Cole's mom's famous apple pie while drinking a cup of Cole's coffee, will all be gone.

The afternoon rush is here, and the cafe is a flurry of activity. People breeze in and out. I've felt a few pats on my arm, and I managed to muster a couple of small smiles when I needed to. But otherwise, I'm sitting here nearly comatose —the sweet sounds of that old familiar music flow from the radio. I've always found it soothing, but not today. Today it hurts.

"Hey," Cole whispers, his mouth inches from my ear. "How're you doing?"

"Apart from wanting to super glue my ass to this seat and never, ever leave? I'm doing just peachy."

He smiles, but there's a sadness in it. One that wasn't there before.

"Give me another half hour and then you and your ass are mine." He nibbles my earlobe and then whisks away to top off someone's coffee.

His words leave me wanting more while simultaneously wondering how he does it. Despite what's coming, he still manages to give me something to look forward to.

He's still living in the now.

Maybe it's time I join him.

When the cafe clears out and only we remain, I lift off of the stool and stalk toward him. His back is to me as he swipes his rag over a table. I move until the front of my shoes meets the back of his. Weaving my arms under his, I grip his waist, pulling his body flush with mine.

"Hi," I croon.

"Hi," he murmurs.

Resting my cheek against his back, I hum. "This is my favorite place."

"The cafe?"

"The cafe, yes, but really, it's just you."

He chuckles, and I feel the deep vibration against my chest. "I'm not a place, Sylvie."

"But you are. You're my happy place. Wherever you are, I'm content as long as I'm with you."

He turns to face me, plunging his fingers into my hair. "I know the feeling."

"Then it's settled."

His face scrunches. "What is?"

"We're going on a vacation."

He pulls back, looking down at me with concern laced in his eyes. "Sylvie, I don't think that—"

"Shh." I press a finger to his lips. "Don't think. You're my happy place and I'm yours, so for the next two weeks, we're going to get lost in each other. And we're not going to think about what's to come until we absolutely have to." I squint up at him, imploring him to agree. "What do you say?"

"I say …" He lets his hands fall at his side and looks up at the ceiling. I brace myself for what I know is coming and decide to let him off the hook.

"It's okay. It was a crazy idea anyway. I don't know what I was thinking." I start to back away, but he grips my wrist.

"Hang on. You don't know what I was going to say."

"I think I do." I shrug.

"Well, you thought wrong." He smirks. "It's not a crazy idea at all. In fact, I think it's the best one you've ever had. I just needed a moment to work out logistics."

"Logistics?"

"Yeah, namely what to do about the cafe. But then I remembered. I own it. So, if I want to close up for two weeks, I don't need to ask anyone. I can just do it."

"So, we're really doing this?"

"We're really doing this." He smiles, tucking a lock of hair behind my ear.

If only for a minute, I let myself forget about what's to come and live in this moment. Two weeks will go by fast, but I'm going to do everything I can to make every second last.

CHAPTER TWENTY-FIVE

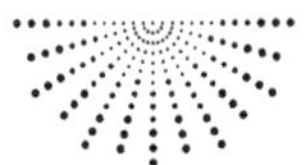

"Am I crazy, Mel?" I ask my friend as I weave through the sidewalk crowd with my phone pressed to my ear.

"Crazy? No, not at all. And maybe that's the craziest part about it. Honestly, Sylvie, it's really romantic."

"It is, isn't it?"

"Mm-hmm," she hums. "You have two weeks left in this fantasy world. Of course, you would want to spend every waking minute together. It's like a fairy tale."

I try to swallow past the lump beginning to form in my throat. "Yeah, except those usually have a happy ending, don't they?"

"That all depends."

"On what?"

"On what your definition of a happy ending is. The way I see it, you've found something most people only dream of. Even if it's fleeting, it still exists. And it will continue to exist long after these two weeks are up. This is the sort of thing people write about and you're out there living it."

"I don't know if all of that qualifies as happy. Sounds more like a tragedy to me."

"Maybe," she agrees. "But the two aren't mutually exclusive. You've got to accept the bad so you can really appreciate the good, you know? And this thing you have with Cole is really good, Sylvie."

"I know that," I whisper.

"So, get your ass to your apartment and pack your bag. I'll take care of everything here in the office. You just go be in love."

"Thanks, Mel." I end the call as I reach my apartment building. I rush upstairs and burst through the door. In a mad dash, I shove everything I'll need into a backpack. Just as I'm about to head out, my phone rings from somewhere deep inside my bag.

"Shit," I groan. I could ignore it, but what if it's Mel.

I fling my bag onto my sofa and root through it, following the sound of the ringtone. My fingers make contact with my phone, and I whip it out, scanning the screen. "Shit," I say again, this time with more of a bite in my tone. It's Aunt Bethany. What could she want? Or better yet, how much does she want?

I sigh and tap the screen. "Aunt Bethany? I don't have much time. What do you need?"

"Oh, am I catching you at a bad time?" When isn't she?

"It's fine. I need to head out in a few minutes, but I can chat for a bit. How are things? How's the new sofa?"

"That old thing?" She chuckles. "Goodness, that was months ago."

The fact that I can't remember how long it's been since we last talked should tell me something.

"Anyway," she prattles on. "I'll get right to it, seeing as you're in a hurry and all. Our TV is on the fritz. Any chance you might have a little extra to spare so we can get a new one? Hmm?"

I always say yes. Always. But for some reason, yes isn't what comes out of my mouth when I open it. "Aunt Bethany, you know I like to help when I can, but—"

"But you want us to buy an even better TV? That's what you were gonna say, right?"

I roll my eyes at the ceiling. "No, actually. Listen, can we talk about this some other time? I need to get going."

"Have you heard from your mother recently?"

Her question comes out of nowhere and stuns me. "I haven't."

"Listen, hun, I know you aren't very close, but she's the only mom you have. You really should be checking in on her, you know?"

"Did something happen?"

"Well, you would know if you called now, wouldn't you?"

She's stringing me along, and I've had about enough of this conversation. "I'll be sure to give her a call myself. Thanks for the heads up. Now, if you'll excuse me."

"All right, all right, cool your jets. She's fine."

I shake my head. "Why did you make it sound like she wasn't?"

She tsks. "I did no such thing, Sylvie. I was just suggesting you should check in on her. Why, just this morning I was chatting with her myself. We talked about you, actually."

I hate myself for the way my traitorous heart picks up at the thought of my mom talking about me. Good, bad, or otherwise. It doesn't matter. Just the idea that I was a fleeting thought in her mind is enough to warm my insides. And I can't help the question that tumbles out of my mouth. "What did she have to say about me?"

"Hmm, let's see." I can just imagine my aunt tapping a manicured nail against her lip as she tries to conjure up the conversation. "Well, we talked mostly about my television. Your mom isn't much for watching shows. Never was. But she knows how important my programs are to me. Anyway, she suggested I talk to you. Said you had gobs of money you didn't know what to do with."

"She did, did she?" I press my lips together. It shouldn't bother me that she sent my gold-digging aunt my way. After all, I'm used to Aunt Bethany's requests. It's more the idea that she assumes I have more money than I know what to do with. She doesn't know how much I make, and she definitely doesn't know how I spend my money. She's never seen my apartment. Never even visited me since I moved here.

"Uh-huh. 'Course, she also said you'd probably tell me no. But you're not gonna say no, are you Sylvie?"

I should. And I was planning on it. But now that I know my mom expects it from me, it makes me want to do the opposite. "I'm leaving for a little trip, Aunt Bethany. But I'll send you money just as soon as I get back, okay?"

"You're a gem, dear. Your mom was wrong about you. You are definitely not a dud. We'll talk soon. Bye bye, now."

The call disconnects, and I'm left still holding the phone to my ear, gritting my teeth. It doesn't surprise me that my mom thinks so low of me. But it's like Aunt Bethany said. She's the only mom I have, and her opinion of me still counts, even if it shouldn't matter at all.

CHAPTER TWENTY-SIX

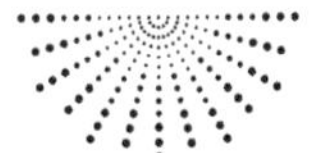

I'm greeted with the incredible aroma of basil and garlic as I glide through the cafe door. "Mmm, something smells amazing."

Cole sidles up beside me, nuzzling his ear against my neck. "Sure does."

I shiver as tiny bumps erupt along my arms. He presses a kiss on my jaw as he takes the bag from my hand. Whisking it away somewhere behind the counter, he calls over his shoulder, "Be right back. I need to go give the sauce a stir. Make yourself comfortable." He disappears into the kitchen, and I take a moment to glance around the tiny cafe.

There are framed paintings of flowers on the walls. Each one looks to be a continuation of the last. A sliver of hydrangea bloom in the first painting sneaks into the second. A bouquet of daffodils takes over most of the canvas, but one leans slightly to the right. The corner of it appears in the third painting. I've never noticed these before, but now I'm studying them like I'm an art critic. Memorizing the long brush strokes and simplistic design.

As my eyes move along the wall, I notice a small crack in

the plaster above the last painting. It's a hairline but continues up to the ceiling. Cole should probably take care of it before it gets worse. I should tell him. Of course, I'll need to do it soon because we don't have much time left.

And there it is—the first of many intrusive thoughts.

This is going to be hard.

"Hey, you," Cole croons. "What're you doing over here?"

I crane my neck, peering back at him. With a wistful smile on my face, I tell him, "Just making a memory."

"Ahh," he says, wrapping his arms around my waist and resting his chin on my shoulder.

We say nothing for several minutes. And the silence says everything.

"Hungry?" Cole asks, his voice breaking through the quiet.

I close my eyes for a second, mentally preparing myself for this night and the ones to come over the next two weeks. There will be no shortage of emotion, but I don't want to spend all the time we have left dwelling on the sadness. When I blink my eyes open, I feel ready. Or maybe I'm just fooling myself. Either way, when I turn to look at Cole, the smile on my face is genuine. "Starving."

COLE IS AN EXCELLENT COOK. It's just one more thing to add to the ever-growing list of how incredible he is.

"Now you've gone and done it."

He flinches slightly. "Done what?"

"You've managed to ruin all other tomato sauces for me." I smirk.

He chuckles. "Have I now?"

"Mm-hmm. I've never had homemade sauce before and

this," I point at my plate with the prongs of my fork, "is divine."

He leans back, looking pleased. "I'm glad you like it."

"It's incredible."

"So, your mom never made homemade sauce when you were younger?"

It's such a simple question. He has no idea how loaded it is. "Psh." I scoff. "I was lucky if my mom heated up a can of SpaghettiOs for me."

He tilts his head. "What do you mean?"

"Oh, sorry, SpaghettiOs are like little pasta shapes in tomato soup. It comes in a can and—"

"No, I'm not talking about that. You've mentioned your parents weren't very involved in your life. Was your mom not much of a cook?"

This conversation is veering into dangerous territory. I could change the subject or brush it off like I did last time, but honestly, I don't want to. I don't have much time with Cole, and spending it talking about my parents doesn't sound awesome, but I want him to know me. And my past is a part of who I am, whether I like it or not.

"Um, you could say that. As I've mentioned, she wasn't your typical mom. Definitely nothing like your mom, that's for sure." I giggle, but it sounds forced.

"Tell me. I want to hear it all. Even the worst parts. Let me be here for you." He leans in, laying his folded hands on the table.

It's a funny thing, talking about your past when it's not pleasant. You do everything you can to avoid even thinking about it most of the time. But when someone you care about asks such a pointed question, it's like a dam releases. You open your mouth to speak, and you suddenly can't stop. Years' worth of pent-up emotion comes pouring out.

"I wasn't planned and I definitely wasn't wanted. My mom as much as told me that herself. My parents met in college. Mom was twenty, and Dad was twenty-one. She had plans to be an accountant. She's really good with numbers. But then I came along and changed everything. My parents got married, mostly out of obligation, though they're still together, so I think they've grown to like each other over the years. Mom dropped out to stay at home with me and Dad finished up his degree and got a job in an office doing what? I have no idea."

"You said she told you she didn't want you?" His mouth pinches like he's tasted something he doesn't like.

I nod. "That she did. Several times, actually. The first was when I was around six years old. I was playing make-believe pretending to be a doctor, and she said, 'Maybe you can be one for real someday so long as you don't have a baby and screw it all up.'"

He shakes his head. "That's awful."

"It is, but it's also the truth, at least, according to her. I'm not saying it didn't hurt when she said things like that, but I knew where she stood and that helped me not get too close to her. I kept myself guarded around her, still do, in fact. And the one good thing is it's allowed me to live my own life without worrying about what she thinks. Because she'll never think anything good." That's not entirely true. I wish I didn't care what she thought, but sometimes, no matter how hard I try, I still do.

"I'm sorry, Sylvie. Truly."

I shrug. "It's fine."

He shakes his head. "But it isn't. None of that is your fault and you certainly aren't to blame for your mother's shortcomings. It's ridiculous for her to make you believe otherwise. And where was your father during all of this?"

"Busy making the money. Too busy for me."

He grits his teeth, looking pained. "I really hate this for you."

"Don't waste your time. Really. It's not worth it. Like I've said before, I've accepted it for what it is. I was a mistake, but I've never lived my life that way. I've just been chasing happiness. Which I'm sure is an extension of the happiness I was denied as a kid." I sigh. I don't like thinking about all of this, but whenever I do, I'm kind of amazed that I've turned out the way that I have. I've somehow managed to stay on the track I mapped out for myself when I was in high school, never veering off even for a second. That is, until I walked through that cafe door.

"You're really strong, you know that?"

My cheeks flush. "I'm not strong. If I was, it wouldn't bother me when my mom calls me a 'dud.'"

His eyes darken. "She said what?"

I shake my head. "It's nothing."

He scoots his chair around until it bumps up against mine. His eyes bore into mine, and he grabs my hands. "Don't do that. Don't diminish your pain like that. You are not nothing. And you most definitely are not a dud. Sylvie, I don't know how a mother could ever say that about her child, and I'm so sorry it happened to you."

Tears pool in my eyes, and a slow blink sends them trailing down my cheeks. There's nothing more validating than when someone acknowledges your hurt. "Thank you," I whisper.

He lets go of my hands and presses his palms just above my knees. Leaning in, his nose touches mine. "You matter. And I'm grateful that you're here."

CHAPTER TWENTY-SEVEN

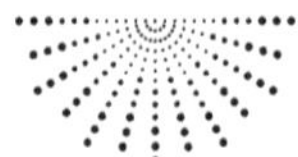

After dinner, Cole and I needed a reprieve from the heaviness of the conversation we'd been having. Cole suggested a walk along the beach.

Hand in hand, we exited the back door of the cafe, crossing the busy street. A two-block walk brought us to where we are now, standing on the wooden boardwalk overlooking the ocean.

I can't stop myself from marveling at the surrounding area. The ocean is in the same place in 1934 as it is in 2023, but the boardwalk is just that—a walkway constructed of wood planks. There are no kitschy shops selling shore shit or snack carts beckoning you with the overwhelming aroma of freshly popped corn. It's simple and more beautiful than I ever could've imagined. The wonder of the area in this century is the ocean itself and not the atmosphere of entertainment that dots the landscape of 2023.

Cole and I step off the boardwalk and onto the sand. I slip off my sandals, and he slides out of his oxfords, taking a moment to remove his socks as well. The sand is smooth and soft on the soles of my feet. I wriggle my toes, feeling the cool granules move between them.

It's low tide, making the beach feel miles wide. We traverse the sand until we reach the spot where the water rushes toward us. Frothy foam bubbles over the tops of our feet. The shock of cold has me yelping. Cole chuckles, gripping me around the waist and spinning me in a circle.

I couldn't tell you if there was anyone else on this beach with us. I only see Cole. And from the way he's looking into my eyes, he only sees me.

He settles me back onto the sand and reaches up, taking a lock of my hair between his fingers. "Your laugh is my favorite sound in the world. I swear I could hear it every day and it still wouldn't be enough."

Cocking my head, I say, "It's your favorite sound? Hmm, that's not what I recall you saying the other night." I catch my bottom lip in my teeth.

He gives my ass a playful smack, eliciting another yelp out of me. "You're a bad girl, Sylvie."

"And what are you gonna do about it?"

He grins. "You'll just have to wait and see."

A warmth spreads through my body at the thought of what he might have planned.

We stay wrapped in each other as we gaze out into the ocean. "You know, we may be centuries apart, but this view is the same for me as it is for you. The buildings and things around us may be different, but the ocean hasn't changed. No matter what happens, when I'm back in 2023 looking out at this water, you'll be here in 1934 looking at it, too. It's sad, but also comforting. Does that make sense?"

The back of his hand brushes against my cheek, and he leans in, pressing his forehead to mine. "Perfect sense," he whispers.

~

WE WALK ALONG THE BEACH, mostly silent, hands intertwined. I think we're both just taking in the moment, reveling in it, committing it to memory.

Wordlessly, we walk from the sand back onto the boardwalk and meander around the town. We stroll past quaint little shops and quiet restaurants. Cole pauses a few times to tell me anecdotes. He talks about a time when he was young and thought a dish of butter was ice cream. "Imagine my surprise when I took a giant spoonful of it! Here I thought I was the luckiest kid in the world getting to have ice cream before dinner." He laughs. "Serves me right, I suppose."

"Oh my God, that's horrific and hysterical. What did your mom say?"

"She didn't say a word. Just shook her head and handed me a napkin." He chuckles softly. "Guess that was a clue that I wasn't meant for the world of fancy restaurants with special silverware."

"I've never felt super comfortable in those places either. I know you're supposed to work your way in from the left, but I'm more of a 'this fork works for salad and for steak and for pie' kind of person."

He bobs his head. "Completely agree. Why complicate things with extra forks?"

"Exactly," I say, giggling.

"Speaking of ice cream. We never did have dessert. What do you say? Shall we head to the parlor?"

"Lead the way, sir."

We resume walking, and Cole leans down so close his lips brush against the edge of my ear. "You called me sir. I liked it. A little too much."

I close my eyes, feeling his words in places I'd rather not feel them in public. Then, with a confidence that surprises me, I look up at him and say, "I could say it again. When we're alone."

His nostrils flare. "I'm counting on it," he nearly growls.

We walk the next block with desire crackling in the air around us. Cole grips the handle of the ice cream shop, but before he can tug it open, I grasp his hand. His eyes snap to mine. "Do we want to maybe skip dessert? Or better yet, we could have it back at your place?"

He looks up at the sky, puffing out a breath, and then back at me. "Sylvie, there's nothing more I want than to keep you locked away with me in my bedroom for the next two weeks. Believe me. But it's important to me to have these moments with you."

I nod, unable to speak for fear of crying. It's crazy how I can go from feeling aroused one second to utterly gutted the next.

Stepping inside the ice cream parlor is a bit like the first time I set foot in the cafe. It looks like the land time forgot, only it's completely relevant for the year we're currently in. There's a man behind a long chrome counter wearing a pointed white hat and a long-sleeved white shirt with a red bow tie. He has a red pocketed apron around his neck and tied behind his back. He smiles warmly when he sees us. "Good evening. Lovely night, isn't it?"

"Sure is," Cole answers, though he's looking at me.

"What can I get for you?" the man asks.

I usually go for chocolate chip cookie dough, but something tells me this place hasn't heard of that. "I think I'll have a banana split."

"A classic," the man says. "Coming right up. And for you, sir?"

As soon as he says *that* word, I bite my lip to keep from laughing. Cole squeezes my hand and whispers, "Behave."

He orders a chocolate milkshake. We find a quiet table

near a window while we wait. "So, tell me, if we were in your century, what would you order in a place like this?"

"Hmm, well, for starters, we don't really have places like this where I'm from."

"Really? Wow. That's hard to imagine."

"I mean, we have ice cream places, but most of them are chains."

"Chains?"

"Yeah, I guess that's not a common word in 1934. It just means that there are restaurants that are the same in multiple locations. So, for us, we would go to Coldstone or Dairy Queen for ice cream. Or we just buy it at the grocery store, which is my preferred method."

"Not much for eating out, are you?"

"Um." I look down, suddenly enamored with my fingernail. "It's not that. It's more just … unless I'm going with Mel, I'm alone. And eating alone is bad enough, but eating out alone is not very enjoyable." He frowns, and I feel the need to explain myself further. "Don't get me wrong. I don't mind being alone. Sometimes, I actually prefer it, but when it's the only option, it gets old after a while."

He nods. "Yeah, it does."

We sit in companionable silence, mulling over the words we shared, knowing full well that alone will feel even worse when these two weeks are up. Because now we'll know what we're missing.

"There you are. One chocolate milkshake, and for the lady, the finest banana split in the entirety of the town." The man with the red bowtie places our order in front of us with a gleam in his eye.

"The finest in the town, you say, huh?" I smile, pressing my lips together.

"You betcha." He makes a show of looking around like he's making sure no one is in earshot before leaning in. "I'll let you in on a little secret. You see, the trick is you've got to drizzle a little of the sauce from the maraschino cherries on top. That way, the flavor really disperses." He stands up straight, nodding once before waltzing back to his post behind the counter.

A tiny laugh bubbles out of me as I reach for my spoon. Sampling a bit of my sundae, I let the flavors linger on my tongue before swallowing. "I don't know if this is really the finest banana split in all the land or whatever it is he said, but it is pretty spectacular. And he might be on to something with his cherry juice addition." I glance up at Cole and find him looking at me, a wry grin on his face. "Why are you looking at me like that? Do I have whipped cream on my nose or something?" I grab a napkin and dab at my nose.

He chuckles. "No, you're perfect. And the best part is, you have absolutely no idea."

My cheeks flush and send my attention to the bowl of ice cream in front of me. "I'm hardly perfect," I murmur.

"See, that's where you're wrong. You don't even realize the effect you have on people, do you?"

I rub a hand along the back of my neck. "What do you mean?"

"Take that guy, for instance." Cole tips his head in the direction of the man behind the counter. "He was completely enamored with you and you didn't have a clue."

I purse my lips. "He wasn't enamored with me. He was just being nice."

"Was he? Do you think he gives everyone who orders a banana split the same spiel he just gave you?"

"Probably." I shrug.

"Probably not," Cole says pointedly.

This conversation makes me uncomfortable. It's true I'm not the greatest at reading people, but having it pointed out in this way makes me feel a little dense. And I'm not sure why Cole is saying these things.

As if he can read my mind—and he probably can because, unlike me, he is very good at reading people—he adds, "Hey, I didn't mean to make you feel bad. On the contrary, I was just trying to point out how incredible I think you are. And how I'm not alone in those thoughts. But I can see from the look on your face that it must've come out all wrong. I'm sorry."

I shake my head. "It's fine. I know you weren't trying to make me feel bad. It's just … well, I sometimes feel a little clueless when it comes to other people and what they're thinking. And I guess you really shined a light on that just now."

"And I made you feel self-conscious," he says softly.

"Maybe just a little," I say, holding my thumb and pointer finger up with a little distance between them.

Cole smiles sheepishly. "That wasn't my intention. I'm sorry."

"All is forgiven," I say with a wink. "Now, are you gonna drink that milkshake or am I gonna have to take care of it after I finish my super incredible, most amazing in all the world, banana split?"

He laughs, and it's deep and wonderful, and it does things to me that no laugh has any business doing. "I'll shut up and drink my milkshake, and then we can walk back to my place."

"That's the idea, sir," I say in my best breathy voice.

His eyelids lower into a slow squint, and his jaw works back and forth. I may not be good at reading most people, but I can definitely read him at this moment. The desire he oozes is almost enough to melt my ice cream.

CHAPTER TWENTY-EIGHT

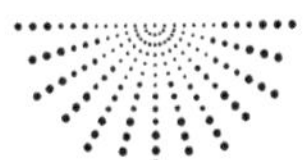

The walk back to Cole's house is brisk. We barely speak as we walk at a clipped pace. Ornate street lamps dot the sidewalk, illuminating our path as we nearly jog the last block.

When we reach his door, Cole takes my arms at the wrists, pinning them behind my back. He walks us backward until I feel the brick I against my shoulders. We stare deep into each other's eyes for seconds that feel like hours, and then he descends upon me, pressing his mouth to mine. I part my lips, and his tongue dives forward, scraping along my teeth. Our breaths are heavy as we explore each other's mouths. I moan against him, and he responds with a growl that resonates throughout my body.

We're on full display in front of his house, but neither of us cares. I lift my leg, wrapping it around his waist, and he catches it with his free hand. His palm moves along my thigh, trailing up until his fingertips brush along the lace trim of my underwear. Just as he's about to touch me where I want him to, he lets go, dropping my leg and backing away.

His chest heaves with ragged breaths as he looks at me

like I'm something he wants to devour. "I can't seem to control myself when I'm with you," he rasps.

"So, don't," I challenge

He stalks toward me, hooking an arm behind my knees and the other at my back, and before I have a moment to react, he hoists me up, cradling me in his arms. He looks down at me with tenderness in his eyes. And then, with a small smile, he walks us to his front door, where he fumbles with his keys and finally pushes into the vestibule.

With a swift kick, he slams the door shut behind him and continues carrying me up the stairs toward his bedroom. I close my eyes for a moment, imagining this is our wedding night. Cole carries me over the threshold and up to our room to consummate our marriage. It feels right in a way, like nothing will ever be this right again.

Oh no, I can feel the tears beginning to fill my eyes. I don't want to cry. There will be plenty of time for that later. Right now, I want to be here at this moment and hold on to it for as long as I can. I blink furiously, trying to clear away the moisture, grateful for the darkened hallway that shields my face from view.

Cole walks us straight to his bed, and in a move, I've only ever seen on the big screen, he lowers me down adoringly, caging me in with his arms. Slowly, he climbs onto the bed, straddling me, all while keeping his eyes locked on mine. I've wanted him before. Many times. But something feels different about this.

Maybe it's the weight of the moment. The way we know our time is nearly up. Or maybe it's because there's more than lust between us. We're not just two people who desire each other. We're two people in love.

And so, I take that love, and I put it all into the kiss that I place on his parted lips. It's not a frenzied kiss. We aren't mauling each other with our mouths. This kiss is soft and sweet and soulful. I feel my chin begin to quiver as my emotions start to betray me. Cole takes my chin between his thumb and forefinger, holding it steady as he presses his mouth to mine.

A few more seconds of this kiss continues before it's more than we can take. We push into each other harder, fusing our mouths like we're trying to fuse our souls. Like if we could somehow connect ourselves in a way in which we couldn't be separated, then we'd never have to leave this moment.

Cole sits back on his heels, admiring me. With hands that move slow and torturous, he slides up along my sides, taking my shirt with him. He sweeps it over my head, and then, in one quick motion, he tugs his own shirt off. They join together somewhere on the floor, and then he lowers onto me.

His lips dot my face in soft kisses that he trails down my neck and into the hollow of my throat. He continues his descent, gliding over each breast and kissing each nipple with nothing but the sheer fabric of my bra between us.

I moan softly and feel his lips curl against my skin. He continues moving down, taking the fabric of my skirt into his fists and balling it up until I'm bare before him with only my underwear separating us. He hovers his mouth where I want him the most, and I can't help myself. I shift my hips slightly, angling myself toward him while whispering, "Please, sir."

"Say it again," he commands.

I keep my eyes on his and suck my bottom lip into my mouth. Releasing it slowly, I plead, "Please kiss me there, sir."

He lets out a sound that's nearly feral as his mouth crashes into me. He nudges me with his nose and swirls his mouth around in a circle. The friction isn't enough. Not with fabric in the way. I release a frustrated groan, and he tsks.

"Now, now. Is that any way to act? Good things take time, you know." He pauses his ministrations for a moment. "Here," he says, hooking a finger into the gusset of my panties and pulling it aside. I feel the warmth of his breath as he moves closer. He swipes his tongue along my core, and I moan in a way that might be embarrassing if I cared. But I don't.

He continues adding pressure and taking it away. It's a dance that's both tortuous and exhilarating. I feel my desire climb as though it were ascending rungs on a ladder. Once I reach the top, I remain there for so long that I think I may lose my mind. With one quick flick of his tongue, Cole shows me the mercy I need as I crest over the edge. The crescendo is loud and long as I writhe and wail.

When I reenter my body and get a grip on my breathing, I look up at Cole and find him marveling down at me. "What did I tell you? You're perfect." He leans down, placing soft kisses along my neck. "Perfect for me," he murmurs. I close my eyes, catching his words and imagining them going straight to my heart, where I lock them up, keeping them with me forever.

With a contented sigh, I press up to my elbows. "My turn," I tell him with authority.

"Is it now?" He grins devilishly.

"It is. Lie on your back."

He cocks his head. "What's the magic word?"

I smirk. "Sir."

He closes his eyes, inhaling deeply. "There it is."

He does as I say, and I waste little time sliding off his pants and tugging off his briefs. He's at attention as I take him in my mouth. Slow and tortuous, the same way he was with me. I let my tongue move in lazy circles over his tip, closing my mouth over his length every so often and catching him off guard every time.

"Jesus," he moans. "You're too good at that."

I alternate between licking and sucking while picking up my pace and suddenly slowing down. Cole's hips rock up and down, and his mouth falls open. I have all the power at the moment, and there's something so incredibly freeing about it. I've never felt so in control.

Before I can finish what I started, he presses a hand on my shoulder. I look up with him still in my mouth. "As much as I love seeing you like this, I need to be inside of you."

I pull off of him in a slow stroke, and he sucks in a breath, shaking his head. "You're gonna be the death of me, you know?"

I chuckle. "I don't want to be the death of you, but I'd settle for being your life."

He lifts up. Sliding a hand along my jaw, he cradles my face, looking deep into my eyes. "My love, you are my entire world."

His words are like napalm. I launch myself at him, catching his lips in mine. No matter how slow we try to be, we always end up frenzied like this. The connection we have is too much for us to take our time.

Cole flips me around so that I'm on my back, and in one quick moment, he thrusts into me. I gasp at the fullness. He begins to move, never taking his eyes off of mine.

Neither one of us speaks the words out loud, though I'm certain we're both thinking the same. How are we ever going to say goodbye?

CHAPTER TWENTY-NINE

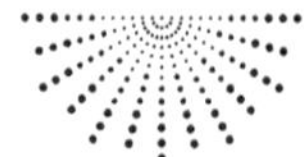

I don't want to wake up because once I do, I'll have to face the last full day Cole and I have together. I knew these two weeks would go fast, but I still feel like we were robbed. Robbed of more time. Robbed of what we could be.

And what we could be is great.

Monumental.

Everything I ever wanted.

How do I say goodbye to that?

"Wake up, sleepy head," Cole croons. I feel his cool lips press against my warm forehead.

Blinking my eyes open, I groan, "Do I have to?"

He knows what I mean. Understands the full weight of those words. But he chooses to ignore them. "It's an incredible summer day out there. And we're going to enjoy every bit of it. Starting with breakfast."

"Mmm. Breakfast? Say less."

He chuckles. "I love how much food motivates you."

My eyes widen. "Excuse me, but have you had your

breakfast? The coffee, the French toast, the eggs, the bacon. It's divine."

"Fair point." He grins. "I just love taking care of you, is all."

I shake my head. "You say that so casually, like it's this easy thing to do."

"But it is. It's the easiest, most natural thing I've ever done. And if I didn't know any better, I'd think I was put here on this earth just to take care of you."

My eyes immediately fill. Shit. Here they come. I could try to blink them away, but they're coming much too fast and furious for that.

"Hey," he coos. "It's okay." He swipes the tears from my face.

"How are you staying so stoic?" I blubber.

"Stoic? Are you kidding? Listen, I'm right here in this with you and if I'm not careful, I'll fall apart completely. I'm just trying to soak it all in. Enough for a lifetime. If that's even possible. I don't want to miss a single second with you." He looks away, a sad smile on his face. "There will be plenty of time for falling apart later." The words are barely audible, but I hear them. And it helps. I don't need him to be a mess of tears and snot, but just knowing he's as affected as I am is enough to get me up and out of this bed. Because he's right. We only have this time together. There's no sense in wasting it worrying about what's to come.

"All righty. I'm gonna throw on some clothes and then you're going to lead me to the food. Sound good?"

He nods, grinning. "Sounds like a plan."

AFTER BREAKFAST, Cole asks me what I want to do, and my response is easy. "Just be with you."

He takes my hands in his. "Be with me where?"

I shrug. "Anywhere."

"I can do that. In fact …" He looks off into the distance with a faraway look in his eyes. "I have an idea."

❦

"THE MOVIE THEATER?" Cole and I stand hand in hand in front of the familiar structure.

He smiles. "This is where we had our first real date. Do you remember?"

"Are you serious?" I say, shaking my head. "I'll never forget it."

He tugs on my hand, leading me toward the ticket booth. "Two, please." As we enter the lobby, I'm reminded of the night we came here. I was so enamored with the ornateness of the building; it was almost overwhelming.

Tonight is different. It's still beautiful in here, but I'm more enamored with my company and less interested in my surroundings.

We find our seats inside the immense theater. "I didn't even ask you what it is we're seeing?"

"*Cleopatra*," Cole answers. "It has the same actress as the last movie we saw, but this film is much different."

"Have you seen it?"

He shakes his head. "I haven't. Have you?"

I'm struck dumb by his question until I remember that we don't exist in the same timeline. In 2023, this movie would be a classic and one I easily could've seen before. I can't seem to find my voice. I look down at my hands, fidgeting in my lap.

Cole touches my chin, turning me to face him. "Where'd you go?"

"You know, it's silly really, but being here with you these

past two weeks, I've almost started to think of myself as living here in 1934 with you. But when you asked me that question just now—"

"It reminded you that you don't," he finishes.

I nod.

"I've been feeling the same way. And if I thought it was going to be hard to let you go before, now that I know what it feels like to be with you every second of every day, I don't know how I'm ever going to let you walk out that door."

The room begins to darken, and Cole turns to face the screen. His throat bobs with a hard swallow.

The movie starts, but I don't bother to look. Instead, I focus on the man beside me. I watch with rapt attention as he takes in the film. I'll have plenty of time to see this movie when I'm back in my lonely apartment. Right now, I'd rather keep my eyes on Cole.

He turns his head, capturing my eyes with his. We hold each other's gazes like we had held each other's bodies every night for the past two weeks. Like we never want to let go.

There's something about being in a darkened movie theater. Everything is amplified. Your thoughts are loud, and your emotions are even louder. And as we sit here watching each other more closely than we watch the film on the screen, so much passes between us. We have whole conversations without ever uttering a word.

I spent my whole life searching for happiness. I was so sure I could find it in my career. I pushed myself to get the degree I needed to get the job I wanted and then climbed my way up the ladder for the promotion I was sure would be the answer. But the truth is, every time I reached a new milestone, I'd immediately find a new one and a new one. Nothing was ever enough. Because nothing made me truly happy.

Until now.

What I've been searching for is right in front of me, and in less than twenty-four hours, I'm going to have to walk away from it.

CHAPTER THIRTY

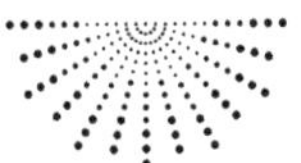

When the theater lights come on, and the ushers filter in with their dustpans, we stand to leave. Our feet move as though they're trudging through bubblegum. Each step is slow and deliberate. We're stalling, and we both know it, though neither one of us would ever admit it out loud.

As we reach the double doors, I take one last glance over my shoulder, marveling at the palace, knowing I'll never again see its equal. Cole catches my gaze, and we share a meaningful look. One that lets me know he feels it too. He may be able to come back here again, but for him, it'll never be the same.

We leave, knowing we're leaving another moment behind.

Once we're outside, I swipe away a few tears. "I hate this," I say through trembling lips.

Cole cradles my cheek, and I lean into his touch. "Me, too."

We stand there on the busy sidewalk, parting the crowd.

People pass by us in a blur, having no idea what's happening between us and the devastation that's about to happen.

It's amazing, isn't it? We go through life seeing strangers everywhere, not knowing a thing about them. We might say, "Excuse me" to the man in the grocery store who just found out his wife is pregnant, or maybe we hold the door open for a woman whose mother just passed away. And we never have a clue. Everyone has a life outside of what they project to the general public. And here, outside this theater that has marked our beginning and end, we are lost in each other, yet these people milling about don't understand. Better yet, they don't care. It has nothing to do with them. This is our moment, and we're only sharing it with each other.

"Come on," Cole says, slugging an arm around my shoulder. "This day isn't over yet."

❧

"THE BEACH. I do love it here." A wistful smile fills my face as I stare out into the deep blue water. The waves crash along the shore, leaving behind a white froth that reminds me of a root beer float.

"Over here," Cole says, tipping his head toward a blanket with a wicker basket in the center.

"What's all this?"

"Just a little picnic I threw together." He half-shrugs, plunging his hands into his pockets.

"When did you have time to do that?"

"Well, lucky for me, someone likes to sleep in." He taps the pad of his finger against my nose.

I grin. "What can I say? I'm a fan of sleep."

He chuckles. "I've learned this about you."

"So, you made a picnic for us, but how'd you manage to get it here? Did you wake up at four a.m.?"

He shakes his head. "No. I may not need as much sleep as you, but I wouldn't want to wake up that early. Plus, I love sharing a bed with you. That time is invaluable. I'd never sacrifice it."

I close my eyes, letting his words settle over me. I've always slept alone, but I've never slept more soundly than these past two weeks.

"Anyway," he continues, bringing me back to the present. "I made the food and my mom helped by setting this up for us."

"That was so nice of her." We've spent most of our time just the two of us, but we did have dinner with his family one night. It was both wonderful and sad. His family is loud and boisterous. He and his brother, David, talk over each other, and his mom makes way too much food. Everyone told stories; most were about John. I was sad that he was away at basic training. I would've loved to have met him. Even his dad, whom I haven't heard much about and the little I've heard hasn't been great, was in a decent mood. I felt like I fit in and it devastated me. It was one more perfect thing about what I have with Cole and one more reminder that it's only temporary.

"Mom was happy to do it. She loves you."

I press my lips together to keep them from trembling.

"Have a seat," Cole says as he lowers onto the blanket.

I settle onto the checkered flannel fabric, tucking my legs beneath me. The basket is something you might see in a children's book. It's made of natural wicker and has two wide handles that lie along each side. The top is tented with hinged flaps that open wide. Cole pries them apart, revealing an exorbitant array of food. He reaches in and begins to lift containers out of the cavern-like basket, setting each one on the blanket until they fan out in front of us.

"That basket is like one of those clown cars. It looks

deceiving like it might hold a decent, but small amount of food. But this is a feast fit for at least a dozen people." I shake my head, marveling at all the food.

Cole smiles sheepishly. "I suppose I may have gone a little overboard. I just wanted this to be special, is all."

I lean forward, placing my palm on his cheek. "You could've tossed a loaf of bread and some butter into that basket and called it a day, and it would still be special. The food isn't what makes this memorable—though I'm going to enjoy eating every last bit of it. It's this time with you that will be seared into my brain. Years from now, I'll think of this moment, and all I'll see is you." I close my eyes as I drift closer. Close enough that our noses touch. I tilt my head, and he bends his, and our lips meet in a soft kiss full of unspoken promises.

High-pitched giggles pull us out of our reverie. We chuckle as we see a young girl no older than four holding her father's hand, trying to jump over waves. Try as she might, each one crashes over her legs before she has a chance to dodge them.

"I wonder if …" I almost say it. Almost mention the non-existent children we don't have. The ones we can never have.

Cole grips the back of my neck, pulling me to him until our foreheads meet. "Me too," he whispers.

CHAPTER THIRTY-ONE

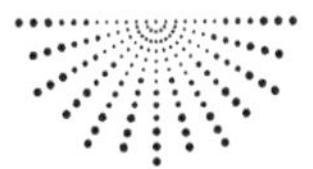

e vowed to stay awake all night. We're down to our last moments together and want to hold on to them as long as possible. We made it until four a.m. before Cole started to drift. He was fighting it, but I told him to give in. As much as I love being awake together, I wanted some time to just watch him sleep. I've been the one to fall asleep first each night that we've been together, and now, on our last night, I wanted to see him in that peaceful state that only happens in deep slumber.

The first thing I notice is how impossibly long his eyelashes are. They feather out and curl slightly at the ends. There's a tiny pinprick of a strawberry birthmark on his left temple and a small crescent moon-shaped scar above his right eyebrow. His face is relaxed except for a slight smile that's barely perceptible, but it's there. Maybe he's dreaming about how our lives could've been.

If I close my eyes, I can see it so clearly; it's as if it's really happened. We're married and living in this little house with our two children. Adeline is seven, and Cole Jr. just turned three. We work in the cafe every day and have dinner as a family each night. Our lives are simple, uncomplicated, and happy.

I don't know how to do this.

I don't know how to walk away from a future I can see so perfectly.

And then it hits me.

What if I didn't walk away? What if I stay?

I bolt upright, taking the covers with me. Cole moans, reaching for them, and when he realizes they're out of his grasp, he cracks an eye open.

I scrub a hand over my face and look down at him. "I figured it out."

"You figured out what?" He sits up slowly, taking my hand in his.

"How to stay," I murmur. My eyes ping-pong around the room as the idea takes root. "Cole," I say, with more urgency this time. "I don't have to leave."

"What do you mean?"

I turn to face him. "What I mean is, this doesn't to have to end. When the bulldozers show up tomorrow, I'll be here with you. And when they break apart the 2023 version of the cafe, I'll be a permanent resident of 1934." A wide smile blooms on my face. I can't help it. The excitement I feel is palpable.

"Sylvie," Cole whispers. "As lovely of an idea as that is, I can't let you do it."

I purse my lips. "What do you mean, you can't let me? Of course, you can."

He shakes his head. "No, I can't. You have a whole life in 2023. One that needs you. No matter how much I wish you could stay here, you need to be in your version of the world. It's where you belong."

"No, where I belong is here with you. How can you even suggest anything different?"

"Sylvie, you have a family and you have Mel. You have a career that you've worked so hard for. I can't ask you to give all of that up for me. I won't."

"You're *not* asking me. It's my idea. And besides, what family do I have? Distant parents and a greedy aunt—wow, what was I thinking? I definitely can't leave them behind. And my career is the thing I *thought* would bring me happiness. Turns out it was only a placeholder."

"What about Mel?"

I sigh. "You're right. Mel is different. I'll miss her more than I can say. But she'd want this for me. She's only ever wanted me to be happy."

He looks down at our joined hands and then back at me. There's a sadness in his eyes that seems to grow as the minutes pass. "Come on," he says, giving my hand a squeeze. "Let's get some breakfast."

"Why does this feel like a permanent subject change?" I tip my head, studying him with scrutinizing precision.

He lifts his eyes to the ceiling. "It's a 'let's get some food in our stomachs before we make rash decisions' suggestion."

"Fine," I groan. "But if you think it's going to change my mind, you're wrong. If anything, your food is a huge plus in the 'I should stay' column."

"Is it now?"

"Damn right, it is."

He chuckles, but I notice the way it seems forced. He's holding back. Looks like I'm going to have my work cut out for me.

BREAKFAST IS a quiet medley of scraping forks and clearing throats. Cole hasn't said much since we left the bedroom. He seems lost in thought, and I've let him have the time he needs. He'll come around. He just has to think it through.

My mind has been preoccupied as well, thinking of all the loose ends I'll need to tie up before I leave the twenty-first century. I originally planned to stay with Cole until late tonight, but I'll need to head out soon if I want to have enough time.

"So," I say, breaking the silence. "I need to run out for just a bit today."

Cole swipes a napkin over his mouth. "What for?"

"Just some things I need to take care of."

"Sylvie, if this is—"

I lean across the table and grip his hand. "Don't worry about it. I won't be gone long. We'll have plenty of time."

He sits back in his chair, looking resigned.

We finish eating and take our dishes to the sink. Standing shoulder to shoulder, he washes, I dry, and I think, even this is perfect. I love my dishwasher, but I would give it up in a heartbeat to have this time with Cole, where even the most mundane tasks feel meaningful.

The walk back to the cafe is peaceful and introspective. I stroll along the sidewalk with an ease I didn't have before because I know soon this will be my neighborhood. These streets will be my streets. This cafe will be my cafe. And I can't fucking wait.

Cole unlocks the back door, holding it open for me. Once we're inside, I turn to him, but he speaks first. "Listen, I know what you're planning, and I really just want you to hear me out."

I cross my arms in front of my chest and nod for him to continue.

"I want you to stay. More than anything else in the world, I want you to stay. But not like this. Not when it means you give up everything, while I don't have to sacrifice a thing."

Pressing my lips together, I study him for a moment. "Let me ask you this. If it was you who would have to say goodbye to this life as you've known it in order to be with me, would you do it?"

"That's beside the point, I—"

"No," I say, shaking my head. "It's the whole point. And you don't even have to answer me because I know what you'd do. You'd make the same choice I'm making because, in the end, it isn't even a choice. It's like breathing. It's the most natural thing in the world."

He sighs, letting his arms flop against his side. "I'll see you when you get back." He leans close, kissing me softly. And then he whispers, "And if you don't come back, I'll understand. Sylvie, these past two weeks have been like a dream and I'll hold on to the memory for as long as I live."

I close my eyes, feeling the meaning behind his words. He wants me to stay, but he's hoping I won't.

I glide across the room to the door, and when I reach it, I want to turn around. I want to look at him before I leave, but I stop myself because that will feel like goodbye, and this is not goodbye.

CHAPTER THIRTY-TWO

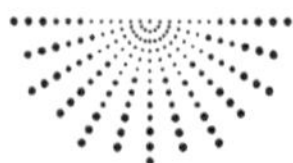

"*M*el!" I practically yell into the phone when my best friend answers.

"Jesus, Sylvie. Everything okay? Wait, why are you calling me? Aren't you staying with Cole until tonight? Oh shit, did something happen?"

She fires off questions at me so fast it takes me a moment to catch up.

"Yes, something happened, or it's going to happen, but, well, I'd rather talk to you in person. Where are you right now?"

"Hang on one sec, Syl." The sound muffles as she puts her hand over the receiver. "Can I please get a Venti Cold Brew with four pumps of vanilla, six pumps of caramel, and sweet cream cold foam on top?" There's a bit of rustling, and then I hear her more clearly. "Okay, I'm back."

"Which Starbucks are you at?"

"The one on Walnut, why?"

"Oh, perfect, you're close. Any chance you could stop by my apartment when you're done?"

"Sure thing. Want me to bring you anything?"

I shake my head even though she can't see me. "No, no, I'm fine. Thanks."

"K, see you soon."

I speed walk the next two blocks to my apartment and rush inside. Standing in the middle of my living room, I survey the space. I never realized how empty it is. I have very little furniture, which makes all of this even easier.

A few minutes later, Mel rings my buzzer. "Okay," I mutter as I press the button to let her in. "Here goes nothing."

"HOLY SHIT, Sylvie. Are you sure? I mean, really and truly sure? Because once that wrecking ball smashes into that building, there's no turning back."

"I know."

"Wow," she says, looking around the room. "Well, hey, at least you don't have much to get rid of, right?" She giggles, but it quickly morphs into tears.

I wrap my arms around her as she cries on my shoulder. My own tears fall in quiet unison with hers. "I'm not crying for you," she hiccups. "I want you to be happy. I've always wanted that. I'm just really gonna miss you."

"Me, too." I sniff. "I wish I could take you with me, but you have a life here. A better one than I ever did. You should take that job, Mel," I say, gripping her shoulders and shaking them. "Move to New York with Curtis. Start over."

She shakes her head. "Oh, I don't know. That's a pretty big move. I don't even know where to begin."

"Let me help."

Her face pinches. "What do you mean?"

I pluck my phone from my pocket. "I've saved up quite a bit of money and I don't have much use for it." I swipe through my apps, pulling up my bank account.

"Sylvie, you don't need to give me anything."

"Nonsense. Consider it a payment."

"For what?" she asks, cocking her head.

I glance around my apartment. "For helping me deal with all of this. I don't really care what happens to anything in here. You can keep it, sell it, donate it—whatever you want. And my lease is month to month, so I'll send off an email to my landlord, terminating it at the end of this month."

"You're really serious about this."

"I've never been more serious about anything in my life. Cole is it for me, Mel. He's my missing piece."

"Then I say, do what you gotta do." She grabs my hand. "He really loves you. The things he wrote in that letter … whew," she says, fanning herself with her hand.

"You never told me what he said."

"And I'm not gonna, but trust me, it's nothing you don't already know. Now you go to him. I'll take care of everything here. Don't you worry about a thing."

"Thank you." I smile at her.

"Oh, and you don't need to pay me for this. I'm doing it because I love you."

"I know you do. And that's exactly why I'm doing it. Because I love you. And where I'm going, I don't need much. Plus, I know you'll put it to good use."

The balance in my account is staggering, which further proves that I'm making the right decision. What good is all this money if you just let it sit in the bank? Mel will start a new life and see the world, and even though my time with her is coming to an end, I can relax knowing she's taken care of.

"I guess you better get packing, huh?" she says as her lips begin to tremble.

I blink a few times, releasing tears. "I guess so."

We reach for each other at the same time, wrapping one

another in a tight embrace. "I'm really gonna miss you, but I'm so happy for you, Sylvie."

"I'm gonna miss you like crazy. But you know, in a world where time travel exists, I have a feeling anything is possible. This is not goodbye. This is see ya later."

THE MOMENT I closed the door after Mel left, I felt a strange calm settle over me. It's hard to imagine my life without her in it, but I know good things are coming her way. She'll live a long and fruitful life. And I'm going to give her a proper send-off so she doesn't have to worry about anything for a while.

I tap away on my phone, and within a few minutes, the bulk of my savings account has been transferred to Mel. I reserve a small amount for my Aunt Bethany, forwarding it to her account. I wonder if I should give her a call, but then I think twice about it. What would I say? "Hi-ya, Aunt Bethany. I just sent you some money because I'll be leaving this year and traveling back to 1934, and I won't be back." I'm sure that would go over super well. I decide to send her a quick email telling her I'm going away and I'm not sure when or if I'll be back. I ask her to check in on my parents and tell them I love them. I recognize how crazy it is that I can just leave forever and never talk to my parents again, but I think it's for the best. Nothing good has ever come from those phone calls. And in the end, I'm giving them what they wanted—a life without me. And I'm surprisingly at peace with that.

I type out one last email to my boss, Allison. I haven't been there for two weeks, and even though I didn't have a plan when I left, I think deep down I did. I finalized everything I had been working on and left all my files in a folder on my computer's desktop. I thank Allison for the opportunity and tell her how much I've enjoyed working with her. And when I finish, I don't feel a single ounce of sadness, and that shocks me more than my decision not to call my parents. Because this job is what I based my entire self-worth on. And now I'm just … walking away like it's no big deal. Which, as it turns out, it isn't.

With all that done, the only thing left to do is pack a bag. I rush around my apartment, grabbing a few outfits and some things I want to take with me, but for the most part, I leave it all behind.

It's time for me to start over, too.

CHAPTER THIRTY-THREE

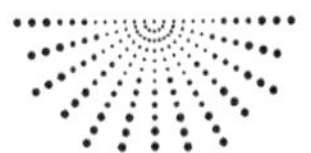

$\mathcal{I}$ take my time walking back to the cafe. I'm desperate to get back to Cole, but as I stroll along the chipped and broken sidewalk, I take in my surroundings, saying a private farewell to this world as I've known it. There are things I'll miss, but nothing I couldn't live without.

I never visited Cole's house in this timeline. It might sound hard to believe, but I wasn't even tempted. I only ever wanted the visual of how it exists in his world. Seeing it in 2023 would alter my memories. And now I never need to worry about that.

I walk with my head held high, confident in my decision. It wasn't a hard choice. It wasn't even much of a choice. I kept looking at this situation as though it just had to end. It took me so long to realize that the goalpost could be moved and "the end" could be the end of me living in this timeline instead of the end of Cole and me.

The sun is beginning to rise as I reach the cafe door. The construction crew has started to arrive, and bright orange traffic cones block off part of the road. Grasping the handle,

I take one last lingering look over my shoulder, giving this century a final nod goodbye.

Closing my eyes, I tug on the door and smile when it opens easily. He left it unlocked for me. Because he knew I'd be back.

The little bell chimes, and I can't help myself; I shove the door closed behind me and quickly lock it. There's a part of me that's sure something will try to pull me back out.

I hear the light tap of shoes on the linoleum behind me. Steeling myself, I turn slowly. Cole stands a few feet away, hands shoved in his pockets, a sober look on his face.

"I know what you're going to say, but this is my life, and this is my decision. I know what I'm doing. I've never been more certain of anything else in my life. So don't try to talk me out of it. I'm not going anywhere. This is where I'm supposed to be."

"Shut up."

My eyes widen, and my head rears back. "Excuse me?"

"You heard me," he says, taking a step forward. And another. And another. Until he's standing right in front of me. He weaves a hand through my hair, gliding it down until he reaches the back of my neck, where he grabs me tight, pulling me to him. "Shut up and kiss me."

His lips quirk into a small, confident grin, and it's the last thing I see before I crash my mouth into his. We move with an urgency even though we have all the time in the world now. The bags I'm holding fall from my hands, landing on the ground with a bang. With my hands free, I wrap them around Cole's neck as he moves his to my back. We lower to the ground, our lips never separating. He lifts my shirt, and his palms trace the curve of my ribcage, setting my skin ablaze. My skirt comes off next, followed by his pants, yet we still stay connected, our lips bruised, swollen, and unrelenting. As Cole moves over me, entering me with slow and deliberate precision, I wonder if we'll be able to hear it. The crash of metal against brick. The broken facade of the old cafe crumbling apart into a heap of rubble. Or will it just happen without us knowing exactly when?

Cole's movements are tortuous as he takes his time. Breaking our kiss, he pulls his head back, peering down at me. "I hoped you'd come back. I didn't want you to give up your life for me, but I wasn't sure how I would continue living without you."

"I know." I moan. "I felt the same way."

"I guess we just couldn't say goodbye," he whispers gruffly.

And then we stop saying anything at all.

He presses his lips to mine, and I feel every promise in that kiss. Before, we existed in moments that we thought would one day be taken away from us. But now we have a lifetime of moments.

Our future is the past, and the past is our future.

"I NEVER KNEW linoleum could be comfortable," I joke.

Cole cringes, but my giggles coax a smile out of him. "I'm sorry, I can't seem to help myself when I'm with you."

"And I'm counting on that always being the case." I wink.

He leans over, capturing my bottom lip in his teeth and giving it a little bite. I squeal, and he laughs low and deep.

"Do you think it happened?"

"Probably," he answers without me having to clarify. The demolition of the old cafe is heavy on both of our minds. "Want me to check?"

I pause a moment, my eyes searching his. "Let's go together."

Cole rises to his feet, holding out a hand to help me up.

We take small steps toward the door, both afraid of what we'll find, but also curious.

He unbolts the door and peels it open. "It looks the same to me, but it always has. Here, why don't you take a look?"

I swallow hard and lean to my right, holding on to Cole's arm like it's an anchor keeping me solidly planted in this century. I expect to see what I've always seen when I open this door. The bustling street filled with people rushing to work. The empty storefront across the street with the faded Space Available sign in the window. I expect to see cars and taxis breezing by going speeds a little higher than they should be. What I don't expect to see is a quiet street with brass lamp posts meticulously placed along the sidewalk. There's a patch of grass separating the walkway from the street, and when I lean further out, I spy two small wooden flower boxes filled with bright orange marigolds placed neatly on either side of the cafe door.

My feet begin to move, taking me out to the front of the building. I hold Cole's hand tight, and this time, nothing separates us as he steps outside with me. The cafe sign looks the same as I remember it, but the building looks different. It's clean and unmarred by time. Even though I wasn't seeing it the way everyone else in 2023 saw it, I still wasn't seeing it the way it is here in 1934. "Your cafe is adorable, Cole."

He sidles up behind me, wrapping his arms around my shoulders. "You mean *our* cafe."

I sigh. "I'm not sure I'll ever get used to this."

"I don't want you to."

I turn my head, giving him a side-eyed glance. "Why?"

"Because, when you get used to something, it becomes trite. Boring. Ordinary. And nothing about our lives together from here on out will ever be described that way."

I hum in agreement.

"I was wrong before, you know." he says.

I narrow my eyes. "What about?"

"Happily ever after. Turns out it does exist." He gives me a squeeze.

I close my eyes, melting into him for a moment. Then I step away, holding my arms out at my sides.

"What are you doing?" he asks.

I answer with a smile, then I tip my head back and start spinning. I giggle like a child at a playground, and I think this is happiness. This right here. This is how it's supposed to feel.

CHAPTER THIRTY-FOUR

MEL

I've accumulated way too much shit in this office. I started working here a few years ago, and from the look of my desk drawers, I just kind of moved myself right in. I can barely get the bottom right drawer open; it's crammed full of what should probably be work-related papers, but it's not. Instead, I find part of my Vogue magazine collection. Bits and pieces of it are scattered all over this space.

And listen, I know what you're thinking. "Mel, you work in this office. When would you ever have time to read an article, much less look at all of these magazines?" The answer is, you would be surprised. There's so much downtime here. Too much.

And now?

I let myself look at Sylvie's office door, but only for a second. I'm so happy for her, but damn it, I miss her. She was right, though. Taking care of her apartment and the contents of her office took no time at all. She was always so orga-nized, or at least, that's what I thought. But being alone with her things these past two weeks made me realize she was unsettled. She was never entirely comfortable, so she never spread out. Everything was neat and tidy and kept at a minimum.

It was all a badge for what she was missing in life. I can't be upset that she chose to follow her heart. After all, that's exactly what I'm doing.

I pack the last few things into a box and close the lid. Giving it a pat, I set my car keys on top and lift it, getting ready to make the last trek out to my car.

Before I leave, I walk across the space, stopping at Sylvie's office door. It's slightly ajar, so I give it a little shove with my elbow. The door swings open. The space is so empty. Totally devoid of life. Sylvie was a bright spot for me here, and now that she's moved on, it's time for me to do the same.

The familiar synthesizer beat of The Weeknd's "Save Your Tears" plays from the pocket of my pants. I let the box slide from my hands onto the empty desk and pluck out my phone. "Hey, babe," I say into the receiver.

"Hey, yourself," Curtis croons. "How's things? Almost outta there?"

"Yeah," I murmur, taking another look around the office. "Just about to take the last box out to my car."

"Almost time, baby. Only ten more hours till we're offi-cially New Yorkers. Can you believe it?"

I shake my head. "I kind of can't."

"Still feelin' good about everything?"

"Absolutely."

"Good," he says, and I swear I can hear his smile through the phone.

"See you soon, okay?"

"All right, baby. I love you."

"Love you, too." I end the call and tuck my phone back into my pocket.

I'm about to pick up my box when I notice a newspaper sitting in the trashcan. It's funny, I don't remember seeing it there before, but I must've been the one to toss it, seeing as I've been cleaning out Sylvie's things. Still, something about it gives me pause. I lean down and snatch it from the trash.

It's from a week ago, which would be odd since our offices are cleaned nightly, but I asked Allison to have the cleaning service hold off on Sylvie's office until I left in case there was something I missed. And now, looking at this paper in my hands, I'm really glad I had the forethought.

At first glance, it looks like an ordinary paper, but under the fold, right on the front page, is an article about the new shopping center. There are pictures of the construction site along with a smaller picture of the cafe as it looked years ago. Standing in front of the building is a man and two women. One looks to be a bit older, maybe in her sixties perhaps. But the other one? I'd recognize that smile anywhere. It's Sylvie. Unbelievable.

I smile wider than I have in weeks. "You did it, girl," I whisper. "You did it."

CHAPTER THIRTY-FIVE

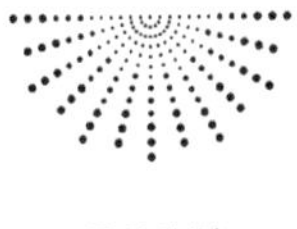

COLE

EPILOGUE

I've never been one to look back or forward. I'm a live life as it comes, kind of guy. Or at least I was. Until I met Sylvie.

I tried to stay focused on the present, but with her, all I wanted was the future. I was sure we couldn't have one, but she proved me wrong.

It's been nearly two years since she first walked through that cafe door. So much has changed since that day.

I asked her to marry me the day after she moved in, and three weeks later, in a small beach ceremony, we were married. We wrote our own vows, and when it was her turn, she looked out at the ocean and told me she was so glad we'd be watching it together. To the few people in attendance, it sounded like a sweet thing you might say to the person you love, but to Sylvie and me, it meant so much more.

We thought we'd be watching that water alone, taking comfort in knowing it was the same ocean we'd be looking at. We never dreamed we'd be getting married here. Planning a future. Starting a life together.

And what a life it's been.

My little house was fine before. It was enough for me, and really, I only needed a place to sleep. When Sylvie moved in, that old house became a home. Somewhere I look forward to going to at the end of a long day.

Our lives together are simple and perfect. We work at the cafe during the day, and when we finish, we usually take a walk around the town. Sometimes we stop for ice cream. Sometimes we see a movie. Sometimes we just hold hands and get lost together. Sometimes we skip the walk altogether and race to get home—our minds on *other* ways to spend our time.

"Well, hello there, Cole," a loud voice booms from the door. I know it's Sam before I even turn around.

"Hi, Sam," I call over my shoulder.

"Say, where's that pretty little wife of yours? You know, your better half?" He chuckles like he's made a super original joke, and I laugh along with him because I'm happy, and I don't give a shit.

"She's just behind the counter. Go on over and say hi while I finish cleaning this table."

Sam hightails it toward Sylvie. He adores her. Everyone does. I don't take it personally because I adore her, too. She's what was missing, and now that she's here, everything makes sense.

I look over at her and smile as I watch her slice a piece of pie for Sam. She moves a little slower these days, taking care of the life inside of her.

With Sam settled, she strolls out from behind the counter and makes her way over to me. "How are my two loves?" I ask, resting a hand on her belly. The moment my palm makes contact, it jolts from a kick. "Wow, quite a little acrobat we've got in there."

Sylvie smiles. "She's just saying hi. She knows her daddy."

"'She,' huh? And what makes you so sure this baby is a girl?"

She shrugs. "Call it a hunch? Isn't that right, Adeline?" she asks, rubbing her hands along her belly.

"Adeline," I murmur. "I like it."

Sylvie wraps her arms around my neck. "I knew you would."

I grip her waist, drawing her toward me. "Oh, you did, did you?"

"Uh-huh." She nods.

"Such confidence."

"Don't worry," she whispers. "I won't let it go to my head … sir."

I close my eyes, inhaling deeply. "You're gonna pay for that," I growl.

"I'm counting on it." She places a quick kiss on the tip of my nose and breezes away, calling out to someone who just walked in.

This is my life with Sylvie. It's simple but never boring. It's easy but never dull.

And most of all.

It's happy.

ACKNOWLEDGMENTS

To anyone and everyone who takes a chance on this book or any of my books, for that matter. I am forever grateful. Thank you.

To my incredible beta readers, Angela and Liz. You guys are amazing. Thank you for always dropping everything for me. Liz, this book would have a lame title if it weren't for you. And Angela, your eagle eye is unmatched. Seriously, who does it better?

To Murphy, we are five for five with book covers! I am forever in awe of you.

To Marla, thank you for polishing my work and catching all of my overused words and phrases.

To my amazing indie author friends. You guys are so supportive and always willing to share and I am just so happy to be a part of this community.

To Adam, this one is for you. <3

To the two halves of my heart, Stella and Jasper. You are my favorite part of life. I am so incredibly proud of the two of you and cannot wait to see where you go in life.

ABOUT THE AUTHOR

Layne Deemer aims to push boundaries with her writing. Her stories deconstruct the ordinary until it becomes something else entirely.

She has a degree in Communications with a minor in English and has worked in the fields of public relations, marketing, and advertising, but writing has always been her true passion. When she isn't writing, she's reading. Her wish list of books will take her a lifetime to get through.

She resides in Pennsylvania with her husband, Adam, their two kids, Stella and Jasper, and their bulldog, Archie.

Other Books by Layne:
Frayed
Life Forgotten
Decompose
Under the Influence
The House on Everly Lane